Scribbles

Scribbles

A Drug Story

Matthew McCain

Library of Congress Control Number: 2018902212
ISBN: Hardcover   978-1-9845-0984-0
               Softcover   978-1-9845-0982-6
               eBook   978-1-9845-0983-3

Print information available on the last page.

Edited by: Amanda Mondugno

Rev. date: 02/16/2018

To order additional copies of this book, contact:
Xlibris
1-888-795-4274
www.Xlibris.com
Orders@Xlibris.com
761707

For you

They say rock bottom is a great foundation to build on. Of course, the asshole who said that probably doesn't even know what the fuck rock bottom is, or even lookslike. Lucky him.

Nope, rock bottom is the saddest, loneliest, most miserable, depressing place you could possibly go. Take my word for it.

But what the shmuck who came up with that clever one-liner won't tell you is; hitting rock bottom isn't as easy as you'd think it would be. First, you have to get to rock bottom. Trust me when I say, the fall to rock bottom is just as bad if not worse than, actually hitting the bottom.

I know all of this because I've been at rock bottom.

Many times actually.

Many, many, many times.

...

MANY!

Looking back, it's easy to judge and figure out where it was that I went wrong, but in the moment, it wasn't as obvious (course, being addicted to cocaine and prescription drugs, probably didn't help the situation, either).

But drugs were only part of it. Everybody seems to think that people just wake up one day and say to themselves: "You know what? I think I'm gonna head out, grab a bite to eat then stop and pick up some crack cocaine from our friendly neighborhood drug dealer."

Hate to break it to you, but addiction isn't that simple. If it was, no one would be addicted to anything. You don't need to spend $200,000 on a fucking law degree to know that (no offense to the poor bastards who have spent $200,000 on said law degree).

Addiction is complicated. It's complicated because of the circumstances that lead you to that point. That's what people get wrong when they're trying to recover. They're so focused on trying to kick the habit, they completely ignore what got them started in the first place.

Now don't get me wrong, DRUGS ARE BAD FOR YOU...but...they do help in getting you to rock bottom faster. Only problem with that is, certain drugs will kill you before you get there (those evil double-edged swords!). I live in New Hampshire, so when I say I've seen it up close, you know I'm being honest.

Nowadays, up here in the Granite State, you have everything from meth to fucking elephant sedative on the street, (those local friendly drug dealers hard at work!) but back in 2009 when I started doing drugs all there really was to choose from was cocaine, oxycontin and pot (lots of pot). It might sound strange, but I'm glad I was an addict back then instead of now because if I was, I probably wouldn't be alive.

My choices were cocaine and prescription drugs. Yes, they aren't good for you, (not to mention kind of illegal and carry a rather stiff jail sentence, under the right circumstances), but they were nothing like the shit today. Of course, that's really not saying much; drugs are drugs no matter how much bullshit you tell yourself.

They may not have carried the same amount of danger today's shit does, but boy do they fuck with your head! I don't care what anyone tells you, you are not the same person coming out as you were going in. That shit changes you; makes you do things you never thought you'd do.

But as fucked up as this shit may sound, in a sense, the drugs pushed me down the rabbit hole much faster than I was originally going. The breaking point was my second (or third) trip to the hospital. I stopped keeping track after two.

I'd love to sit here and tell you that it all got better later that evening after I left the ER and that everything was fine, but I'm not here to feed you shit. See your local shrink for that, so they can tell you how much they understand and sympathize when they don't even know what the fuck is wrong with you. Yes, the sun may have come up the next day, but the fuck-ups were still there, waiting.

But I digress…

Anyway, flash forward 5 years and here I am: diagnosed with Rapid Cycle Bi-Polar, ADD, and sitting in a dimly lit room at two in the morning writing all this shit down. But, as anticlimactic as that sounds, it's actually the best part of the story. It's the best because I have one thing that I never had in all those years: peace.

I can look in the mirror now and be proud of the little fucker who looks back. It wasn't very long ago when I couldn't even look up at him (small victories!). Back then I couldn't see it, but looking now I see battling drug addiction the same way as I see someone going into the military: you grow up fast, you risk your life, you lose friends along the way and most of all: you change.

I don't remember a whole hell of a lot of those drug-filled days and probably never will either, but one day, about a month or so back, I was doing some cleaning and came across a journal. This little black, yellow-paged journal, about the size of a pocket bible.

I have no idea where the fuck it came from, (or who even gave it to me for that matter), but when I looked inside, it felt like someone hit me with a 2x4. Inside there were pages and pages of what was clearly my chicken scratch handwriting, dated and all. I was beside myself because none of the dates were recent.

All were dated back years ago.

And here I sit hardly remembering writing a fucking word.

I had always wanted to be a writer ever since I was in fourth grade (hell, I even started writing screenplays before I reached high school), but I always thought that part of me was lost, like everything else was, because of the drugs. I guess not.

I sat for hours on end reading what was inside. Reading through the misspelled words, reading through the scribbles.

And since I have nothing better to do, I thought I'd share them with you.

7/14/2012

11:17pm

This is the beginning I guess. The beginning of another long journey. There's a good chance that I'll never write in this fucking thing again, but I think I'm going to try.

Today was my birthday party. 20 years old. I must've invited 15-20 people. But only 1 came.

I don't have many friends. Don't have any brothers or sisters. It just me. Sometimes it gets lonely. Lots of times it gets lonely. Days like this I could call up Tyler and ask for a little snow.

But can't

Mom said a long time ago I have to go to a hospital if I ever did drugs again. I haven't in couple months now. I don't know if prescription drugs count as drugs. If they do, I'm fucked.

Writing in this fucking thing is boring. What's the point? Therapy my ass. This fucking shrink Dave Ledner is useless. Fucking tells me I have Bi Polar. Non one else has it in the family!

Mom just has depression and my fucking father was just abusive and mean all the time. Don't miss him. Glad I don't see him. 6 years next month. I'll kill the prick if I ever see him again.

Ledner says I should write in this every day. Even said he wanted to see them. Fuck him! No point! The guys useless and so are the meds he gave me.

Funny: everyone got mad when they found out I was stealing sleeping pills and shit and now they want me to take pills. That makes a lot of fucking sense. Bunch of hiprocrats.

Well as fun as this was I'm gonna end it here. Thanks for nothing Ledner and thank you to all the people who didn't show up today. Means a lot.

Fuckers!

7/17/2012

Hell froze over

Never thought I'd be back here.

Board I guess. Out of Oxy too. That's why God invented spiced rum and sleeping pills! Haven't done that combo in a while. Last time I did that, woke up in a puddle of booze.

Gross

All over my clothes. Had work early too. Needed to clean it up quick before mum came in and found out I was drinking again. Don't need to deal with that shit again.

Goddamn car has another problem. Check engine light on again! Piece of shit. Thanks for the car Nana and Grandpa!

You think after fixing it so much grandpa would just get me a new car! Nope, while everyone else gets to have trucks and motorcycles, I'm stuck with the fucking oldsmobile.

Bullshit

New meds don't work for shit. Still feel the same as I always do. Unreal. You tell people you don't feel good and as soon as they found out you're a druggie they want nothing to do with you.

People suck. They judge before they even know me. Wish mum never found me. Should've fucking died last year. But no, had to make a big scene and take me to the ER. I'll never forgive her for saving me! Jeffrey to! Not even my father and trying to help out.

Would've been quick to! Don't even remember passing out. Would've died in my sleep. No pain. Should've never been the best man at the wedding. Maybe they would've gotten the hint then.

Still not sleeping either. Got up at midnight and listened to music and stared at the wall until it was time to go to work. What a great life! Now I remember why I started doing drugs.

I still have Tyler's number. Really thinking about giving him a call. Maybe then I wouldn't feel so fucking depressed anymore.

Today marks 3 years since my first visit to the ER from a drug overdose. Should've died then to. Sometimes I wonder if maybe I wasn't faggot, my life would be better. Guess I'll never know.

;

Getting through the first few pages was no picnic. After reading each word, those old feelings I left behind years ago started coming right back like they had never left. Actually, I don't think they ever did.

Like I said the handwriting was god awful, but from reading it, it was painfully obvious that I was still miles away from being anywhere close to stable. The sporadic topics going back and forth clearly prove that I was in a manic state of mind when I was writing it.

I had been diagnosed with Bi-Polar earlier that year, by Ledner, after my second (or third) hospital visit. I was required to either see him or I'd have to be checked into Shutter Island. So I ended up choosing Ledner. Of course some days it was hard trying to remember why I chose him instead of the padded room.

I knew something was wrong with me. Even back then I didn't deny that. It's hard to explain, but somedays I would wake up feeling like I wanted to beat the ever-loving shit out of small farm animals, and then before the end of the day, I had no energy left and would be in bed by 7:00. That started in high school (just like everything else does).

I hid it well back then, though. I should've won a fucking academy award for my acting over those years. Not one person thought anything was wrong. Not even my family. But every night, I could feel it getting worse.

I never slept. At all. I was tired as fuck and had no energy, but every time I tried to go to bed: nothing. My mind was all over the goddamn place. I did everything I possibly could to try and fall asleep. I tried staying up later, thinking that would help, I jerked off before going to bed, I did EVERYTHING, and still, NOTHING worked!

I think a lot of it had to do with the fact that I was suffering from undiagnosed Bi-Polar, but there's no doubt that much of it was because I hated that I was gay. No question.

Remember, this was back in 2009. Gay marriage and relationships weren't seen the same way as they are today. It was scary back then if I'm being honest. I was already fat and getting made fun of, and I knew being gay was just going to add more fuel to an already out of control fire. Being gay was also the first reason why I started to think about suicide.

That was when I turned to over the counter meds for help.

Now you have to remember when all of this was happening, a teenager was still allowed to walk into a store and buy a whole bunch of cough medicine and sleeping aids without being looked at twice (how I miss the old days). So when I would pick up bottles of cough medicine or over the counter sleeping aid, no one thought anything of it. I didn't either. I figured if you could get it without a prescription there was no issue, right?

WRONG!

Yes, it worked at first. Yes, I started getting some real sleep and even started to feel somewhat better, but that was short lived. Originally I had started off taking three sleep aids and one measuring cup of cough medicine every night before bed. It was effective, but slowly over time that one measuring cup turned to two cups and those three sleep aids turned to four...then five... then six (I'm sure you can see where this is going).

At first, I just went with the flow and kept adding to my bedtime cocktail. The more I took, the more I was able to sleep, but that sleep started turning into blackouts. That's when the real fun started!

The way my house was set up, my mum and stepdad had the entire upstairs floor to themselves and, I had the entire finished basement, which had a large living room, a good size bedroom and a door to the backyard. So basically I had a good amount of space I could call my own and didn't have to worry about anyone coming down.

I told you all that to tell you this: when the blackouts started they were minor. Some mornings I would wake up on the couch not remembering I fell asleep there, other times I would be sleeping on my bedroom floor instead of in my bed. Pretty harmless at first, but when it got to the point where I was taking an entire bottle of cough medicine with a huge handful of sleeping aids, the blackouts turned into something completely different.

The first major blackout I had was the first night that I drank an entire bottle of cough medicine. Since cough medicine actually contains a rather large amount of alcohol, you could say it didn't mix well with the tons of sleep aid pills. I woke up on my living room floor, completely naked. My clothes were nowhere to be found, the T.V. was still on and I was lying in a big puddle.

I had pissed myself.

The puddle was massive and smelled horrible, but I was so drowsy that I didn't even get up right away. I must've laid in that puddle of piss for over an hour before I had the energy to get up. It was great (NOT!).

Now some will say waking up bare ass naked, in a puddle of your own piss with no memory of it might've been a sign to slow down a bit; I guess I don't fall into the category of some.

I saw it as a little strange, but I was able to shut off all the depressing shit in my head and fall asleep therefore it's okay.

Most teenagers are stupid. I was no exception.

I thought things were going great! Yes, I was blowing through cash like crazy, spending much of my paycheck on cough medicine and sleeping aid, but it was working! The depressing, borderline suicidal thoughts being blurred out I thought was a win!

It wasn't.

The blackouts only got worse, and they only prolonged those suicidal thoughts for so long. They came back hard, too. Abstinence makes the heart grow fonder (I think) is the saying.

I started looking up online ways to commit suicide, specifically painless ways. I botched enough shit in my life, the last thing I wanted to do was fuck up dying. People already thought I was stupid enough.

I spent hours and hours every night searching through some of the darkest spots on the web, trying to find ideas—most importantly directions—on how to properly commit suicide while listening to some of the most depressing music on the face of the Earth.

As stupid as it'll sound, I took my time doing research on suicide. I was scared; not because of dying, but because I didn't want to rush into it, and somehow survive just to be a fucking vegetable for forty years. YUCK!

The problem with waiting to do it right meant I spent more days living (obviously). That was a problem because this was around the time when I started having feelings for one of my friends at school.

Not just little feelings either.

I literally tried every single thing I could to avoid trying to feel that way for him, but it was a waste of time. The hardest thing the human heart can do is let people in…and let people out.

Now maybe you're sitting wherever the hell you are reading this and saying to yourself:

"It's just love, what's the big deal?"

Or

"It's just high school, stop being such a pussy!"

And believe it or not, I would be the first one to agree with you.

But 'gay love' is much different than 'straight love'.

I know some will argue saying that the only difference is that I like dick up my butt-hole, but there's more to it than that.

A shitload more actually (no pun intended).

Maybe only those in the LGBT community will understand, but even though I knew I was gay, I couldn't say it to myself. I know that sounds strange but it's true: when I was home alone and looking at myself in the mirror, I couldn't say those three words to myself.

"I like cock."

...

Just kidding. It was actually:

...

I. AM. GAY.

I tried for years to say it. I slowly started to be able to say it in my head, but never out loud. Not even when I was alone. And if you can't say it to yourself, then there's not a chance in hell you'll be telling anyone else, either.

Like I said, it's a lot more complicated than just liking penis instead of vagina or vise versa. It turns into fucking quantum physics when you start throwing in transgender stuff, but since I don't know shit about any of that, I'll stay away from that.

Basically what I'm saying is this: being gay sometimes sucks and not in a good way. There's a lot you need to get through before it turns into anything good. Or to put it bluntly:

Love is messy.

So if you add up undiagnosed Bi-Polar depression, being a closet case, and the beginning stages of drug abuse, you get...

ME!

You really do. And that, boys and girls, is how drug abuse starts.

7/21/2012

WHY THE FUCK AM I BACK HERE!

Every other person my age is off having fun, clubbing, drinking, parting and here I am in a dark windowless basement writing in a fucking stupid ass journal for no fucking reason!

Why cant I just be normal

This that really so fucking hard to ask for?

Nothings changed since last time

WORK STILL SUCKS

LEDNER STILL SUCKS

NEW MEDS STILL SUCK

LIFE STILL SUCKS

EVERYTHING SUCKS!

EVERYTHING!!!

;

Now I'm no expert, but I think it's fair to say that I wasn't particularly very happy on this day (just a hunch).

I don't remember writing a fucking word, but I still remember feeling that way, and I can even remember why.

For those who have the benefit of not being prescribed prescription drugs (and nowadays I'm sure there's very few), you might be thinking that when you start on a new medication it's supposed to suddenly work and you're good as new the next day. Well, I hate to break it to you, but that is a total crock of shit. Don't feel bad though, I thought the same thing.

Judging by the date on the entry, this was just a week or two after Dr. Ledner prescribed me medication. so that means I wasn't feeling any different because they hadn't been in my system long enough (he might've mentioned that, but I was so busy admiring all the dead planets in his office to really pay attention).

I didn't know it at the time, but certain medications can take up least two weeks to fully get in your blood system and since I fought for the better half of a week to not take them, I still had a way to go before any type of light at the end of tunnel could be spotted.

The handwriting was fucking horrible, so more than likely I must've written it at night. Looks like I wanted to say more but fell short. Bummer, I'm sure it would've been something beautiful too (sarcasm in case you didn't catch it).

If my piss poor memory serves me correctly, this was also around the time when I was starting to have problems on the work front. You see, after high school, I had every intention of going to college down in Florida to start, what was supposed to be my film career, as a famous Hollywood director!

That idea died the summer I graduated.

I was already neck deep in drugs and alcohol long before that summer. I had this great idea that I would make sure I go to school every day, get perfect attendance, and do everything I could to get all A's. I was going to be that kid that stood out and was on the way to making something of himself.

And you bet your ass I did!

But…not in a good way.

I got suspended the very first day of senior year for 'showing up to school drunk'.

Which was total crap.

I did NOT show up to school drunk!

I got to school FIRST and then I got drunk.

…

I told you I was gonna be honest.

Now, to be fair, I can understand if someone went to the principal and said I smelled like booze because I had polished off half a bottle of vodka before the first bell, but that's not what happened!

According to the principal: "A neighbor saw me drinking and got concerned", which was a total cr, ock because I wasn't drinking out of a fucking vodka bottle, I was drinking out of a Poland Springs bottle. I may be dumb, but not stupid.

I had thrown the water bottle out, so there was no 'evidence', but I knew I probably wouldn't have been able to pass a breathalyzer, so I had no choice but to come clean.

That was a fun day. I got suspended and sentenced to AA before the bell rang for lunch. And that set the stage for the rest of the year. I had only squeaked by my senior year, and by the end of the summer after high school, I knew for certain that the Hollywood director idea was DOA.

So I settled for the next best thing: working in a produce department.

Okay, maybe not the next best thing, but one road leads to another.

Anyway, the meds were still not working, I still felt horrible all the time and all that started to affect my 'job performance', if we wanna call it that. The thing with Bi-Polar is that sometimes things are good (sometimes even great) and you feel fine.

Then there are other times.

At the start of taking all the new meds, I wasn't really carrying my own weight. Not to mention I requested like every Saturday off and became really unreliable, so I do share blame for that. However, my boss back then, a guy by the name a D.J. was a fucking miserable, lowlife, piece of fresh green baby shit. In other words, I was not a fan of him.

You could say we really didn't see eye to eye on everything.

It got worse when I let it slip that I had Bi-Polar. Suddenly after that little bit of information got leaked, my hours went from 20 to 8.

Now, this guy D.J. would fuck his co-workers in the backroom where fresh fruit gets cut for our loyal customers, but I guess mental illness is where that cock smooch draws the line in his moral authority. It kind of sucked too, because, for a brief second, I actually thought he was a nice guy. Two faced people, gotta love them.

The cut in my pay was also a big bullet to take. It got a little scary there for a while, but I had made some friends during the months I had been working with D.J. and they were able to move me to a different location in the company. I spit in his coffee on my last day of work and had to privilege of watching him take a huge sip before I left (karma is a fickle bitch, my friends).

I made a promise when I first started seeing Ledner that I wouldn't f have any type of relapse, and if I had any of those feelings, I had to tell him immediately.

I broke that promise.

D.J. had been known as an asshole, but I couldn't help but feel like the reason why he pushed me out was because of who I was.

Feeling like you're a problem, much like a third wheel, is a shit feeling. That's how I felt. And that's why I chose to take two steps back after just taking a step forward.

I had never gotten a new cell phone after high school, so I still had all my contacts at that point. So that night I chose to go through them and find one that I should've deleted a long time ago, but chose not to.

After passing nearly a dozen names who I couldn't remember from a hole in the wall, I got to the number I had been trying to avoid for so long: Tyler.

We had met in gym class back when I was a freshman. He was failing nearly every class, but he always showed up for gym saying it was 'his favorite class. I don't remember how or why we started talking, but that doesn't matter. It's what happened after that does.

He lived in the heartland of the city of Manchester, New Hampshire: The West side. Some of New Hampshire's finest criminals and lowlifes come out of that area. Tyler said his folks were some of those people, and that he would end up being one of them, too.

He was right. He started doing drugs before I even met him, and started selling just after.

I don't care what people say or what you think, Tyler was a good guy. Yes, he sold drugs and fathered a kid he never met, but when I was at my lowest point, he was there.

He used to say 'this world is fucked, and so are we'. I believed that then, and some days I believe that now. But no matter what he was back then, he was a friend when I had no friends. He listened—even seemed to care, and that reason alone is why I'll never look at him as a bad guy.

While I never told him about being gay, very early on in our friendship I told him that I had fallen for someone that I know I could never be with.

Whether he read between the lines or not, I'll never know, but he was supportive. He owed me nothing and yet he listened to my bullshit every day. If that doesn't make him a friend, then the world is a lot more fucked up than either of us thought it was.

When I started having trouble sleeping, he was the one that suggested I try over the counter shit. And when that idea stopped working, he was the one I went back to. I told him that what I needed was sleep. He begged to defer.

"Bullshit, what you need is to get your mind off things," he shot back at me as I sat in his shithole apartment after midterms.

That was when he introduced me to oxycontin. "Try one of these tonight and see how you do."

I had no fucking idea what it was, and now that I think back, I don't think I even asked. He promised me it would work and I took him at his word and tried it that night.

Boy did it work!

Talk about cloud fucking nine! I never asked him if I should just take it alone or with my normal routine, so I just assumed I'd take it with everything else. And that's exactly what I did.

Oxycontin, cough medicine, and over the counter sleeping aid.

What could possibly go wrong with that?

There's a small space in between taking the pills and passing out in a puddle of your own piss that is amazing. It lasts only briefly, but the feeling is incredible. I remember it like it was yesterday.

Everything felt light. My head was like a cloud, my feelings were finally at bay and my emotions were nowhere to be found. It was like floating through space with no sense of time and nothing but the universe in front of you.

I laid on my living room couch, staring up at the effects of the strobe machine I bought years back, listening to music and I was just gone. What followed would be life-altering, but that first night was something on its own.

I wish to fuck I could sit here and tell you what everyone else tells you about prescription drugs, but I can't. That feeling—that place where your mind goes, is incredible.

It's unexplainable.

It's addicting.

That night stayed with me from then until that night in July 2012. It was with me as I made that call to Tyler telling him I was back as a customer, and sometimes it's still with me today.

Even right now.

Tyler had what I asked for. I drove and picked it up the next night.

Like I said before: one step forward, two steps back.

9/3/2012

Looks like I heading to jail or at least the funny farm
Fucked up like always.
Got taken to the ER again. Don't remember much, either.
Tired of shit
Done
Over
Giving up
Wont be a next time
Bye

;

Short and sweet.

As I'm sure you might've guessed from the previous page, I had officially reverted to my old evil ways and went right back to being a regular customer of Tyler's. I saw him at least three times a week, so basically my paycheck was gone long before I even got it. In all fairness though, Tyler would give me a discount most times (friendship right there!). And I did every single thing I could to squeeze out as much cash as possible to give Tyler.

I stopped filling my gas tank.

Stopped buying food during break and lunch.

Stopped buying cat food.

And worked as much as I possibly could.

If memory serves me correctly (keyword is IF), I would normally take home about $330 each week. Since I was still living at home and had no bills of any kind, most of the money would go to Tyler. If I had to guess, he normally got around $290- $300 of my paycheck (might come as a shocker, but drug addiction is expensive boys and girls).

Looking back, I nearly shit myself thinking about how much cash I would blow, but to be fair back then I didn't give a damn.

I JUST WANTED THOSE FUCKING PILLS!

And God bless him, Tyler always delivered. Some weeks he might've fallen short a few, but he made up for it the following week. I remember getting a $200 bonus in my check one week, and as soon as I cashed it, I drove straight to his house without even telling him I was on my way. That was around the time he found out his girlfriend was pregnant, and he was more than willing to take the extra money.

Call me an asshole all you want, but the pills worked. Every night my mind was tame, relaxed and drifting out in the middle of nowhere, like a ship lost in space. The suicide thoughts were nowhere in sight and I loved it!

I more than loved it. I FUCKING loved it!

Every night, those magical little pills took all the shit of the day away and kept me sedated. Sometimes, if I didn't have to work the next day, I would double up on them and take a few more sips of cough medicine.

Boy was those nights fun.

The morning after wasn't though.

I would wake up and feel like I had been hit by a fucking shovel. It was awful! The blackouts were no better. I fell into a coma-like state no matter what I was doing or where I was. I could've been sitting on my couch or taking a shit on the toilet, it didn't matter. When that shovel hit, that was it. It was lights out.

You can't wake up either. You could have an EF 5 tornado pulling your house off its foundation, and you still wouldn't wake up. That was another one of the perks of being a drug user: Sleep!

I'm sure at this point you're probably pissed at me because you're thinking I'm trying to make drug addiction sound fun. WRONG!

As fun as it is to blow your entire paycheck for some magic beans that blast you into outer space before turning you into a fucking zombie an hour or two later, there's actually a downside.

You see there's this little thing called: TOLERANCE

And believe it or not, over time you start to build up said tolerance the more you take those magical pills (that take you to outer space before turning you into a fucking zombie an hour or two later).

Now, for the folks who are still a little lost, allow me to explain: When you first start taking the magical pills (that take you to outer space blah blah blah) you start with a small dose. Maybe you only need one pill in order to get to outer space. BUT over time, one pill isn't going to be enough to get you there anymore.

You're going to have to bump up to two pills.

Then that'll work for a while, but then before you know it, you need to take three.

Then four.

Then five.

Then six.

You get where I'm going with this.

But that's how drug addiction goes from bad, to worse, to serious, to 'Houston, we have a problem'.

It happens over time which is why by the time you realize what's happening, it's too late to stop or go back because you're already there. And when you're at this stage, it starts to get scary.

I hit my peak at seven pills a night. Combine that with cough medicine, suicidal thoughts and prescription sleeping pills that Tyler was able to get his hands on, and you have yourself one hell of a chance of not waking up the next morning…period.

But I never thought about it. Of course, at this point I could hardly think at all, my mind was in places I can't even describe—it was like being in a fucking Stanley Kubrick movie. But I didn't care, I just wanted to keep taking more. And that's what I did.

It took me a little while to realize it, but at some point I had stopped passing out right away and started roaming around, completely unaware that I was even up. The first time I knew something was up was when I woke up and my bedroom was rearranged, and not just a little either. My entire entertainment center was moved to the opposite side of the room and my bed was facing a completely different direction.

I thought someone had broken in (can't help but laugh at that now). It took a little bit, but eventually, I was able to scrape together a few bits and pieces in my head and remembered parts of moving my bed. Still, I thought nothing of it.

You're probably shrugging your shoulders and asking yourself: "How is moving furniture around such a big deal?" Well, that's a great question because I actually asked that myself back then and my answer was: "It's not! A little strange, maybe, but not a big deal."

No, it's not just a little strange, it's actually pretty scary because THIS TIME it was furniture. It may not be furniture NEXT TIME. And guess what? It wasn't furniture next time. It was suicide.

;

The shittiest thing about suicide, aside from actually doing it, is that it never goes away. It's always there and it always will be. Time takes away a lot of things (damn near everything if you think about it), but it doesn't take that away. If you have ever really (and I mean REALLY) considered committing suicide, you'll understand what I mean.

There are two types of people who attempt suicide: those who nibble on the barrel and those who pull the trigger. There is no in between. There are just some scars you get in life that will never heal, no matter how hard you try to forget.

Love is one of those scars.

Friendship is one of those scars

And surviving suicide is one of those scars.

I know this because I was one of those people.

I *am* one of those people.

I pulled that trigger.

As the weeks passed by, and I was taking the pills, I stopped taking the medication Ledner prescribed cold turkey. I could feel the oxy working, and therefore figured I was all set and didn't need the other shit. I had proved

Ledner wrong and felt obligated to let him know next time I saw him that he doesn't know his elbow from his hairy asshole and everything he says is a crock of shit. I FINALLY PROVED I WAS RIGHT!

Nope.

Not at all.

In fact, I couldn't have been more fucking wrong. It would take years before I would know just how wrong I really was.

At first, it was just the basic: spending hours on end looking up ways to commit suicide, and constantly thinking about it. I would also fantasize about what it would be like after I was dead, and thought about how people would react. Those thoughts made me feel better, almost like it would be reminding people of just how popular I was. Of course some days, that would change to feeling like no one would miss me and I would be nothing more than a blip on the radar.

But as dark as that shit sounds, it only got darker.

I started to think about cutting myself. I read online that cutting does many things, from making you feel better to actually killing you. I was, still am, a baby when it comes to getting physically hurt in any way, I freak when I get a fucking paper cut.

But I was confident I wanted to try it, so I started off slow. I did have access to several knives and box cutters, but I kept thinking they would hurt too much. I hesitated for a while, killing yourself isn't as easy as you'd think. One night, I was walking around before I blacked out for the evening and stepped on something hard and sharp.

"Fuck!" I remember shouting.

I looked down at the bottom of my foot and saw this little tiny piece of glass sticking out. The piece must've been the size of a fucking freckle, but boy did it bleed. After pulling it out, I kept pressure on it for a while before it finally stopped.

But as much as it bled, I realized it didn't hurt as much as I'd thought. In fact, after the quick prick of the skin, it didn't hurt at all. That's when I got the idea to try using glass.

I had a bunch of picture frames in my man cave displaying things from awards I got back in middle school, to pictures of when I was little. They carried a lot of memories, but that didn't stop me from punching out the glass in every frame.

After the second frame, my hand started bleeding and again it didn't hurt that much. So I just kept punching and punching until all were without glass, ruining the pictures, memories, and awards inside with each hit. When I got to the last frame and punched that one out, I remember feeling sad because there was nothing else to hurt me…until I looked down. Collecting on the carpet where all the pieces of glass, lined up in a scattered row with several larger pieces still intact. I started punching those.

Over and over.

When the pieces started getting too small, I punched the carpet as hard as I could, then started to twist my fist into the bits of glass, pushing the pieces deep into my skin.

Blood started dripping onto the floor and down my wrist. I must've blacked out after because I remember nothing else after that. I do, however, remember the mess on the floor I had to clean up the next morning. I didn't really do a good job, but it was good enough to hide any signs of what I had done.

I just checked, and if you look very carefully on the carpet, the stains of blood are still there. Like I said; time takes a lot, but not everything.

;

I got over my fears on cutting myself quickly after that and before I knew it, I graduated from glass to box cutters in a matter of days. Knives came even faster. It's going to sound horrible, but I was smart about it. Since it was still the ass end of summer, there's was a chance that it could still get warm even into early fall (gotta love New England weather), so I knew to stay away from any visible skin. It would raise questions if it was 90 degrees outside and I chose to wear a fucking turtleneck.

I started with my upper legs since I had no intention of walking around the house naked. I wasn't able to press firmly down and cut at that point, so instead, I would swing the blade down fast to cut myself as quickly as I possibly could.

It took a while to make contact with the skin, but eventually, I got there. Call it mind over matter, but I always thought that swiping as fast as you could was a lot less painful than doing it the other way. Course any way you slice it, you're still cutting up your own flesh, so there's a chance that theory is a total crock.

It stung more than anything else. The next morning it would hurt a bit, but nowhere near as bad as I thought it would. After thinking about what my father did to me when I was younger, slicing through your flesh seemed almost like child's play.

As the summer passed, each night got worse. More cuts, more blood, more pills. Sometimes I would wake up the next morning surprised as to how many cuts were all over my legs and shoulders, or how much blood was on the bedsheets, but I didn't do anything about it. I just kept going.

One of the worst times was when I woke up one morning and started getting out of bed. My jaw nearly dropped when I saw how much blood was near the bottom of the bed. My sheets and blankets were covered in crusty thick blood. Not going to lie, that was probably one of the scariest moments of my life. I really thought that I was covered in someone's blood.

And I was, only I just didn't realize it was my own.

It took a second to wrap my head around what I was looking at, but once I lifted my blankets off the rest of my legs and felt a sharp pain, my heart sank. The blood was coming from my leg, but it was from a much different spot than normal. I'd be lying if I said I wasn't confused at first.

The blood was coming from a large deep slice across my left ankle. In all honesty, it was a rather horrifying sight to wake up to, and the pain was unlike anything I had felt before. I was dumbfounded as I sat on my bed watching the blood ooze out of my ankle, and drip onto my bedroom carpet. I had no idea what the fuck I was looking at. It got even stranger when I got off the bed and saw a pocket knife in the middle of the living room floor with bloodstained fingerprints all along the blade and handle. It was like being in a fucking 'Saw' movie.

It tookk a little soul searching and time for me to retrace my steps, but eventually, I would find out that I attempted to cut my foot off. No, I didn't believe it either, but my Internet history about cutting off limbs, and the bloody knife made it pretty hard to think it was anything but a coincidence.

Thinking about it now, I can't help but think how much of a fucking idiot I was. To this day I have no fucking idea what my intention was, or why I chose to stop in the middle of it and go to bed. Maybe after a while, cutting my leg off get boring? Your guess is as good as mine.

Anyway, the pain was nearly unbearable for days. When my sock would rub up against the massive wound, I would nearly die.

IT WAS FUCKING AWFUL!

AWFUL!

It took a good long time before that pain went away. I'll tell you what, I've done a lot of stupid shit where I ended up getting hurt, but that definitely stands out in the top ten.

Now, you would think attempting to cut your own foot off with a pocket knife would be that tipping point where you look yourself in the mirror and say: "You know…there might be a bit of a problem, here."

Nope.

Not for me anyway.

As disturbing as trying to cut my own foot off was, that wasn't the tipping the point.

;

I do have to admit that the days following my attempted amputation, I decided to pump the breaks a little, flesh wounds have a way of doing that… most times. I didn't completely stop taking pills, but I did slow down a bit. At this point, I would normally take seven Oxy's, at least half a bottle of cough medicine, and sleeping pills if Tyler was able to get them.

The "break" lasted about a week or so before I started to pump myself back up, only this time oxycontin wasn't what I ended up focusing on, it was the sleeping pills.

While I still asked Tyler for Oxy, I pulled back a bit because he was able to sell the sleeping pills for less money. I got more of a quantity too (win-win right there!).

Maybe it was mind over matter, but I felt like the Oxy didn't really work without the cough medicine and over the counter sleeping pills. It took somewhat longer to get that feeling I so desperately craved. The over the counter shit was able to close that gap (and very effectively to I might add).

It stayed that way for a few weeks, but as summer came to a close, hours at work got cut and I took a hit. Typically, most weeks were around 30 maybe even 35 hours if I was lucky, but that got slashed to around 20.

Now some of you might be saying:

"It's ten hours! So fucking what? Get over it and stop making such a big deal about it, you fucking pussy!"

Well, allow me to explain why those ten hours are such a big fucking deal:

At the time I was making $10.00 an hour, so let's do the math together:

10.00 X 35 hours = $350

After taxes, you're looking at around $310- $320 left in your pocket.

Now let's take away those "only 10 hours".

$10.00 \times 20 = \$200$

After taxes, you're looking at less than $170.

Now take that $170

Subtract food and gas, and guess how much is left?

NOT FUCKING MUCH!

So when I say those ten hours are a big deal, guess what: THEY'RE A BIG DEAL!

Now take the joke amount of money that's left, and apply the drug addiction to the EQUATION and what does that leave you with?

Desperation. That's what it fucking leaves you with.

And do you know what happens when someone is desperate?

ANYTHING! They will do anything and everything during that period. I did anything I could to get my hands on those pills. I used up all my money in my savings, sold DVDs, CDs, my father's wedding ring; I did everything I could. Tyler did the best he could to get to the lowest price he could...but it wasn't enough. I got desperate fast and work showed no signs of picking up.

Withdrawal is one of the worst things an addict will ever go through, and I was heading towards that iceberg fast. When I used up the last pills I had, I started taking dozens of over the counter sleep aids and cough medicine mouthfuls at a time, hoping to pass out, but it was only postponing the inevitable.

The chills came first, hitting me almost without warning followed by a runny nose and cramps, unlike anything I've ever felt before. I had no fucking energy to do anything, sometimes I couldn't even fucking move. It took every ounce of energy I had just to make it to work.

Sleep was gone, too. Before I knew it, I was right back to where I started—lying in bed, in a puddle of sweat, with my thoughts racing like a motherfucker. But it was the chills that were nearly unbearable. I could've been burning myself on a hot stove and I'd still be shivering.

Those nights were long, painstaking, lonely. Nearly seven billion people on Earth, and during those moments, I couldn't have felt any more detached from the world. It was not an easy time. Then again, drug addiction never is.

The days that followed only got worse, and I knew I was going to need something in order to make it to my next paycheck. Panicking, I tried to come up with a scheme to ask for money, but my favors from my mum and stepdad ran dry back at the first ER visit, so I knew there was nothing there. But while brainstorming for some bullshit excuse to get money, an idea popped into my head while I was looking through my mum's bedroom for cash.

She, much like myself, was prescribed many drugs for issues that she had. When I came across them in her room, even I was surprised at how many bottles of pills there were.

I picked them up, one by one, each name as hard to pronounce as the next. Nothing on the bottle said what they did, and I had never heard of any of them, so since I had the house to myself I took them all downstairs and started looking them up online.

Some were for blood pressure, another was prescription Ibuprofen (I'll be dipped in shit if I can remember what any of the others were for), but when I typed in the name of one of the last bottles and the information popped up on my computer screen, a rush of adrenaline shot through me.

It was a generic sleeping pill!

SCORE!

I was happier than a pig in shit. I was borderline cheering with joy! It was like I suddenly got a second wind and felt like the doom and gloom feeling I had been stuck in had vanished.

I dumped them all out to claim them for myself.

Then I put them back in the bottle.

I couldn't just fucking take all of them and hope she wouldn't realize they were gone! Any idiot (or addict) knows that! You have to compensate for the missing pills. And that's exactly what I did.

I poured them all out again, counted them to see how many were in the bottle, and when I had the number, I went into the bathroom to dig through the medicine cabinet for anything that resembled the sleeping pills.

The pills were these little white fuckers, so almost anything would be able to pass as them. I settled on some aspirin that was the exact same color and size. I counted out as many as I needed, carefully slid them into the empty bottle, and put it back upstairs in her bedroom.

Addiction makes you do things. Things you never thought you would or could do. I didn't see it then, but now it's painfully obvious just how serious my problem was. I never even thought twice about taking those pills when I found out what they were, and that's what I think bothers me the most. Never once did I ask myself how it would affect her, I was just out for myself like I had been for so long (too long).

Looking back, there was a chance for me to realize what I was doing was wrong, and to stop myself from becoming THAT person. It wasn't there long, but it was a chance to do the right thing.

I didn't take it, though.

I became that person.

And stole her medication without hesitation.

I knew right away that Mums sleeping pills were much stronger than the ones Tyler was supplying me with. I took a few with a mouthful of cough medicine and I was fucking gone.

They kicked in so fast, I didn't even have time to prepare. I don't remember much during this time, either (can't imagine why). It's all a blur, almost like someone picked my brain and scraped out most of the memories, leaving only little flashes that make no sense.

I still didn't give a shit, though. I just kept taking more and more every night, drifting in and out of the black hole forming in my head. I'd be lying if I said I wasn't willing to stay there forever. But while I was pushing myself closer and closer to a potentially fatal overdose, my folks upstairs were starting to get suspicious.

;

"Stop falling asleep!" I remember my mum shouting at me as she slapped my face in the back seat of my stepfather's car.

Again, I don't remember much, but man were those slaps fucking hard! I could feel my face turn a deeper shade of red with each one! But as hard as those slaps were, they had very little lasting effect because, aside from two or three of them, I don't remember anything else.

The next time I opened my eyes, I remember laying on a cold-ass table, surrounded by a bunch of doctors, with bright fucking lights shining down on my naked body. I have no fucking idea of how I got from the car to the hospital, how my clothes got off or how I was brought into the ER and even after years of trying to put the puzzle together, it's still as blank as ever.

The light over me was nothing short of blinding, almost as if someone found a crack somewhere in the floor of Heaven. I was still drugged out of my fucking mind, but the beam of light was bright enough to keep me from completely drifting away.

The doctors would talk to me, then I'd pass out.

I'd try to answer them, then I'd pass out.

The same thing over and over for I don't know how long.

But as fucked up as I was, I remember the next part like it was yesterday and as clear as day.

After waking up from another blackout, I remember this male doctor standing over me and rudely start asking me questions (I clearly ruined his night). At first, he asked me something about what I had taken, and how he could find out everything by taking certain tests or some shit like that.

I paid no attention, I didn't know what the fuck was going on! The last thing I was going to do was smile and chat with this pissed off doctor while my junk was hanging out on the table! But he was persistent, to say the least.

Over and over he kept asking "What did you take? What did you take? What did you take?" I swear towards the end I was about to scream…but I blacked out again and when I woke up he wasn't talking to me anymore (so I guess it worked out well then, right?).

NOPE!

When I woke up again, that pain in the ass doctor walked back over to me and told me he needed a urine sample. He also said that if I was unable to provide one, he was going to have to use a catheter in order to get it. Again, being drugged out of my mind, I must've told him (and thought) that I could take a piss without any help.

I don't remember the rest of the conversation, but what must've happened was the doctors all left the room and gave me the chance to try and piss in a cup. Thinking this was no big deal, I moved my legs and hopped down off the operating table.

I fell. My legs were fucking jelly and so limp, I couldn't even support my own body weight. I had no strength in them whatsoever. And to top it all off…I couldn't piss, either.

While I laid there face down on that cold hard operating room floor, I remember this feeling of dread coming over me, almost like the drugs were starting to wear off just enough for me to stay lucid and realize the shit storm I was in.

I blacked out again.

This time when I woke up, I was back on the operating room table, with five or six doctors towering over me like some sort of fucking science experiment. I couldn't have been out for more than four or five minutes, but it was just enough for me to forget what I was originally supposed to do when I got off the table.

One by one, they took hold of me from all sides, as I felt one doctor spread open my legs. I felt a cold draft of air blow up on my genitals. I was confused and borderline panicking. The doctor between my legs (unsure if it was the same one as before), looked up at me and said: "The more you struggle, the more it's going to hurt."

I was lucid enough to ask him what he was talking about, but before he answered, this unbelievable, agonizing pain (pain that can't be put into words) shot up into the middle of my penis.

I screamed.

...

Then I cried.

...

Then I sobbed.

I could feel the doctors holding me down as I tried to resist; tried to get out of their grip, but I had no strength. I was lucky that I was able to move my arms and legs. In the end, all I could do was sit there and cry as the catheter slide up inside.

I felt the doctor's grips loosen as I blacked out again.

;

It was her sniffles that woke me up. It took time for my eyes to adjust to the spotlight shining down on me, but once they did, I saw the outline of this woman with runny makeup and messy hair, in a pair of worn out sneakers and grey sweatpants.

My heart, or what was left of it, sank.

I started crying again as she walked up to me and took my hand and looked down at me with heartache. She looked the same way I felt inside; hurt, alone, and confused. We didn't say anything to each other at first. We just looked at each other, watching the tears roll down our faces.

I sat there naked and exposed with nothing but the sound of my tears hitting the metal table and the heart rate machine, but in those brief seconds, I slowly came to the realization that I had completed my journey of self-destruction.

On that night, in that moment, in that ER room, I found rock bottom. And I knew it, too.

Rock bottom isn't your first drug deal or your first hit. Rock bottom is lying naked in the middle of an ER room with charcoal between your teeth, the cops waiting outside the door, a catheter running up your dick, and your mum looking down at you completely heartbroken because she now sees just how lost you really are.

We stared at each other for what almost seemed like a lifetime. I gave some thought to talking first, but she beat me to it (yet another thing I regret to this day). I may have been fucked in the head, but there was so much I wanted to say to her, but I just couldn't find the strength to say it. I did my best to focus on her when she began talking, but yet again I wasn't strong enough and I fell back asleep and don't remember a single word she said.

When I was first born, they had to rush me out because I wasn't breathing, meaning my mum never got to even hold me and say hello. She said that waiting to find out if I was okay was one of the worst things she ever had to go through. Who would've thought twenty years later, she'd be placed back into that same position. I had flatlined in the ER, twice, but I think no matter what would've happened to me, the look of pain on her face would've been the same.

;

The next time I woke up, I was in a hospital bed with a nurse changing my IV bag. She must've seen me open my eyes because she started talking to me right away, asking me how I felt and if I knew where I was. I feed her the normal bullshit lines, kept my answers short and sweet, hoping it would make her leave faster. I just wanted to be alone.

"Someone up there must like you," I remember her saying to me.

"Huh?" I grunted.

"When you were in the ER, your heart stopped. Thought we lost you there for a second. Think you might have a guardian angel watching over."

I shrugged it off, the whole nearly dying thing wouldn't resonate until days later. "Lucky me."

The room was windowless and I didn't have my cellphone. I had no idea what time, or even what day it was, to be honest. Each time waking up from a blackout felt like I was just coming out of a coma. Everything felt dead inside.

It would take a while before I was able to leave, but by early morning, I had my clothes back and was sent home after taking questions from multiple doctors trying to figure out what the hell had happened.

Leaving the hospital is a bit of a blur, too. I can't remember putting my clothes on, but I remember my mum and stepdad helping me into the back of the car and parts of the drive home.

A large part of me just wanted to go home and sleep for years, not just because I was tired, but also cause I knew the conversation I was going to have with them once I was up and moving. I remember feeling sick to my freshly pumped stomach just thinking about it.

We got home just before the sun came up. Instead of going downstairs to my bedroom, my mum put me in the spare bedroom at the end of the hall. I know we must've said something between the hospital and putting me to bed, but I can't remember what (and maybe I don't want to know, or maybe it's something I already know, but just don't want to admit).

She gave me a glass of water and tucked in me in. I fell asleep instantly.

;

I slept as long as I possibly could. Every time I heard the bedroom door open, I would pretend to be sleeping. If there was a way for me to have stayed in that bedroom, I'd still be there.

It was official:

The drugs had worn off.

Back to reality.

I must've gotten up just before noon and wobbled my way into the bathroom. My head was wicked heavy, and the sun coming in through the bathroom window killed my eyes. But even if my head was on straight, and I could remember the night before, nothing could have prepared me for the aftermath of having a catheter.

I screamed at the top of my fucking lungs!

It felt like acid was burning its way through my dick as I pissed. From the first drips to the last drops, I groaned in complete agony and was absolutely speechless from the pain. I tried stopping and hoping it would go away, but holding it in only made it worse. I tried it a few times, but in the end, all I could do was push through until it was over.

After I was done pissing acid, I headed out to the living room where my mum was. She was sitting down in front of her laptop, clearly looking around online. The look on her face had changed drastically from hours before (she didn't even have to say anything; I knew just by her expression on her face).

At first, she allowed me to say nothing. All she said was I needed help and that she was going to send me somewhere, even warned that she left a message for Ledner, demanding I get placed somewhere.

I took it all in.

I didn't fight, nor did I try to change her mind. There was no reason too. I had ruined the second and third chances she had given me, and there was nothing to make her think that I was suddenly going to change.

I listened to everything she had to say and went downstairs to reflect on things I couldn't change. I remember paying no attention to the fact that my man cave had been ransacked. My clothes were thrown everywhere, along with my couch cushions and even my mattress. It looked like I had been fucking robbed.

When I got to my bedroom, I sat down on my tipped over mattress and started crying. I knew this was worse than anything that I had gotten myself into before, and felt there was nothing I could do.

I couldn't deny it anymore…

I needed help.

I had known that for a while, but it wasn't until then that it sank in. And it was strange because for once, it was actually pretty easy to say, unlike every other time I tried to.

Even though mum had turned the fucking place upside down, I knew she still hadn't found my remaining stash of pills. I knew that because the cross they were hiding in was still hanging above my bed. It seemed almost ironic.

Once I gathered enough energy, I reached up and took it down before lifting the top half off, revealing the secret compartment behind the stainless steel Jesus figure.

Not many were there, but what pills were left were still hiding. I took them out and hung the cross back up. I must've stared at them for a solid hour, trying to figure out where I was going to go next.

You always hear about this point in life where you find yourself at a crossroads that will decide what the future will be for you, but since that mythology is thrown around so much, no one believes in that shit. Nobody thinks it's real. I know I didn't. But seeing isn't always believing, sometimes believing is seeing, and as I looked down at those last few pills, I was seeing.

Whether it was because I was tired or tired of hiding (or maybe even both), the idea of taking them never crossed my mind and I'm proud that I can honestly say that. But I knew something needed to be done with them and chose to do something.

After mustering another burst of energy, I grabbed the pills, got to my feet and headed upstairs towards the bathroom. I could hear mum moving around inside, so I knocked on the door.

"What?"

When she opened the door, I walked in right passed her, and over to the toilet. And when I made sure she was watching, I pulled the bag of little white pills out of the pocket of my shorts and poured them into the bowl.

Then I flushed them.

I took my time looking up at my mum, not because I was ashamed, but because I wanted to watch and make sure the pills were gone. Finally, when I knew they were, I looked up, forced out a smile and decided on the path I wanted to take.

"I need your help, mom because I can't do this on my own."

"You won't have, too," she smiled.

I hugged her, explained what was going on, and we agreed to keep no more secrets from each other. I told her I couldn't promise her that I'd be perfect, but I promised I would try. She said she could live with that.

Neither of us said it, but we both knew the next couple of weeks and months would be hard. But for the first time in a long time, after talking to her, I felt like I had something that I hadn't had in a while:

Hope.

And sometimes that's all you need.

9/5/12

I'm an addict.

I fucked up last night, but I'm going to do what I can to make it up. But it well be hard. But Im going to try.

Don't think Ill have to go to the hospital place as long as I'm honest.

Poured all the pills down the toilet and deleted Tyler's number from my phone. Can't promise I'll write in this thing everyday but I'm gonna try.

I don't know how long this is will last. I'm hoping for a while cause I have no chances left. I wish I could go back because there's so much I'd change. Maybe I can find a way to make up for it though. Going to see Ledner this week. I'm actually looking forward to it. Never thought I'd say that.

Maybe next time I write in here I wont be a addict anymore. Doubtful.

But maybe. Find out soon.

Until next time.

PS cathaters fucking hurt!

;

I don't remember shit from the previous night, but I do remember writing this, and how I felt when I was writing it; Dead.

Even though I was a drug addict, no one trusted me, still had charcoal in between my teeth, and I cried every time I pissed, I felt good. Almost like a second wind and that maybe the situation wasn't as bad as I thought it was going to be. I soon learned that was a crock of shit, but for the rest of that day, it certainly felt real.

The days that followed, I was watched like a fucking hawk. It seemed like every other second, mum was coming down to see how I was or if I had taken anything. She even went as far as turning the light on and checking to see if my pupils were dilated. I would get pissy, but she was kind enough to remind me that I had no say whatsoever and that I was still one step away from either going to the psych ward or being kicked out on my ass (tough love, I guess).

I listened and did everything I had to, but it wasn't long before I started getting those feelings again. To my amazement, the first night after that wonderful trip to the ER wasn't so bad, I guess the whole dying on the table thing seeped in a little. But the second night was something much different.

At first, I tried to keep myself busy playing video games, watching movies (yes, including porn you sicko!) and listening to music. Out of all of those things, music was able to offset the drug cravings (though the porn was a very close second).

But it was only a band-aid. At some point the song ends, the music stops, the dude climaxes, and silence takes over once again. And that's when it starts turning to shit.

Those horrible goddamn chills came back with a vengeance, along with the shaking, and the fucking runny nose. What energy and hope I had on the first day was lost by the end of the second night. I tried falling asleep, and when that didn't work, I got up and watched TV.

Nothing helped though, the urge was too fucking strong no matter what I did. I kept trying to replay my hospital visit in my head over and over, to remind me of what I was risking, but it was an effort that failed flawlessly.

And before I knew it, I caved and gave in.

I had thrown out the stash I had hidden in the cross hanging in my room (yes, I know I'm going to hell), but when I started using, the cross wasn't my first hiding spot. In fact, I had MANY spots because I would constantly move them every night. Paranoia is a fascinating thing.

I started searching the spots I could remember and put the whole idea of staying clean on hold for a second.

Mum had ripped the place apart pretty good, but even I knew she didn't search everywhere. She may have searched low, but she never searched high. When I first started using, I would get so paranoid that I would hide everything up in the ceiling (a trick I learned from my father, but that's a story for another time).

Determined to fuck myself, even more, I stood on the recliner, and carefully moved one of the ceiling tiles. I then reached in and started feeling around. Just from the noises, I could tell that my cat, Callie, was also up in the ceiling (despite trying to cover the opening that was on the other side of the basement), but I paid no attention to her, I was on a mission!

Suicide mission, maybe, but still a mission nevertheless, and I wasn't going to fucking stop until it was complete!

DETERMINATION!

I did my best to balance on the recliner, but the fucking thing was flimsy, at best. I could feel dust, cobwebs, insulation, and mouse poop, but nothing that resembled a plastic bag of magic drug pills. When I felt pressure on the ceiling tile and whiskers rubbing against my hands, I did my best to push Callie away.

"Move…move!" I shouted. "Move you little son of a bitch!"

She wouldn't budge. I tried to carefully push her, but she weighed so fucking much, I couldn't do it with just one hand. So without thinking, I lifted my other hand up into the ceiling, reached in and finally grabbed her. Then very carefully I started pulling her over towards me.

I had every intention of yelling at her when I got her out of the fucking ceiling, but just as I got her to the opening, the ceiling tile collapsed, hit me in the head, knocked me on the floor, and sent all the dust, insulation, and mouse poop raining down on me like a mid-summer rain, into my face and mouth.

I gagged, trying to spit out as much mouse poop as I could.

It was fucking disgusting!

After vomiting into the sink on the opposite side of the basement, I headed back up into the ceiling.

…

I found them.

;

I must've sat on my couch, covered in mouse shit, for nearly an hour just staring at the handful of pills. God only knows how old they were, and what might've happened to them the whole time they were up there, but that didn't stop me from desperately wanting to take them.

But unlike every other time where I would just swallow them without thinking twice, this time I hesitated.

Like REALLY hesitated.

…

Hesitated in a way that I had never done in the past.

Don't get me wrong, it took almost all the energy I had to resist swallowing the likely expired pills, but it took just as much to give in.

Again, I was at that crossroads thing I mentioned earlier, and it was up to me to decide where I was going.

I thought about the past.

Thought about the future.

Thought about the mouse poop in my hair.

I thought about a lot of things.

To this day it was one of the hardest decisions I've ever had to make, but I knew I needed to make it. And so I did.

I popped a pill. Then another, and then another.

Then, I popped the rest of them and took a sip of water.

Then, I spit them all out on the floor, and I started balling my fucking eyes out.

I dangled my head over the couch, watching my tears land on the floor, and watching the white pills fizzle into the carpet, while my mind raced in every direction. I must've stayed there looking down at those pills for hours, and ended up falling asleep around 2:00 in the morning.

I had just taken the first step towards beating my addiction.

I couldn't have been more nauseous.

;

I remember getting up after hearing mum getting ready for work upstairs. I thought about telling her what I had done, even felt almost obligated too, but in the end, I chose not to. It would've been a much different story (and probably not one I'd be writing about right now) if I had taken them, but since there was nothing to hide, I figured there was nothing to tell. Never told anyone about this, actually, now that I think about it.

I vacuumed up what was left of the pills, took a shower to try and clear my head, then attempted to fix the ceiling tile with superglue and tape (It worked! The broken tile is still there to this day! I'm looking at it right now, actually).

It would be a crock of shit if I said this was an easy time. It wasn't. Back in high school I was relatively popular (mostly because I would say or do stupid things, but popular nevertheless) and had a lot of 'acquaintances'. But when I got into opioids, I isolated myself from the rest of the world, and over time it was almost as if I had been forgotten.

The friends that were there at one point were gone; many of them had moved on to adulthood and were either starting up careers or starting up a family, in some cases both. While I was happy to see them grow up, it left me feeling more alone. It was like I had just dropped from the sky, and was starting all over again.

It was hard.

Some days very hard.

It took a long time to get back even half of what I chose to throw away. It took even longer to accept that I would never get it all back. Life doesn't wait for you. I learned that early on.

As hard as that was to cope with, most days it was overshadowed by the constant urge to relapse. The nights only seemed to be getting worse, and the withdrawal shit was fucking horrible, to put it lightly. Some nights while I laid in bed wishing I was dead, I started thinking I should've asked for help instead of trying this whole "cold turkey" thing, but I didn't want people to think I was weak; I worried about that enough because of the whole gay thing. I wanted to do it myself.

That first week felt like a decade. I was a fucking zombie; I must've only got two hours sleep at most. It wasn't fun. But I kept charging on as best as I could. My only real hope was that when I went back to see Ledner, he would be able to come up with something that resembled a valid plan.

I was skeptical, but at this point, it was all I had (what the fuck does that tell you?).

I kept diving into music, hoping it would make the nights easier. It did help, but still could never stop that feeling I would get around 12-1 in the morning when it seemed like time would stop so I could reflect on all the shit of the day. I fucking hated that! Still, do.

And just think, it had only been three days since I had been in the hospital. Thinking about that still to this day annoys the piss out of me, but like I said before, sooner or later time takes it all.

In this case, it was later.

9/14/12

Still an addict.

Saw Ledner today. Spent like two hours in his office, but it felt like forever. He went over my lab from the ER. I would've been fucked if mum hadn't helped out at the hospital. I know I owe her big time.

I told Ledner I hadn't taken any of his meds for a long time and that when I was on them, I didn't feel much different. He gave me this big lecture on 'the dangers of stopping medication suddenly'.

He told me to start back on them and prescribed new ones. I don't remember what their called, but theres a bunch.

I didn't tell him about anything else though. I like that he doesn't ask questions.

Start the meds tomorrow. Lucky me.

It's strange.

They treat prescription drug abuse with a prescription drugs.

Amazing what one piece of paper does.

Probably wont be back here for a while. Have nothing good to say anyway.

Bye

;

"They treat prescription drug abuse with prescription drugs". That's probably the truest fucking thing I've ever written down. It's funny that I saw the irony of it even back then like I do now.

I'd laugh if it wasn't so fucking sad.

The entrees were getting longer and they weren't as sporadic as previous ones, which says to me I was somewhat alert and not the fucking weirdo who wrote the last couple of times.

I was there. Unlike the past few pages.

Now, this is the part where I'd like to sit here with a big fucking smile on my face and say that I took the meds, they worked, everything suddenly got better, no one died, everyone lived happily ever after and I can finally end this fucking book.

. . .

. . .

But I can't.

I know. I'm sorry.

Trust me I wish I could (it's not like writing this crap is fun).

But unlike the movies, life doesn't just end with a credit scroll and you assume everyone lived happily ever after. Life is a little more fucking complicated than that.

I knew walking into his office that he was going to put me on something, there was no getting around that, but the thought going on a medication after just getting out of the ER from a medication didn't sit well with me. Granted the meds Ledner were gonna give me were legal, but it was still the principle of the whole thing.

That week after my second (or third) trip to the ER was exhausting just trying to keep my mind off the fact that I wanted those magic pills. But the fact I was able to stay clean for almost a week was unbelievable! Hell, an hour felt like a fucking accomplishment. So when I was told that I'll be going back on medication, it felt like a catch 22 and a kick in the balls. Like the whole week and mental struggle to stay away from pills had been for nothing.

Getting past that and understanding the difference was a big pill to swallow, but I knew I had no choice. I kept reminding myself it was either Ledner or a straight jacket. There was no in between.

;

I didn't fully understand it then, but if I was any other person I wouldn't have had the chance to go home that night after. You'd actually have to go to the funny house for a certain amount of time (I think it's like 72 hours or something), but I was able to squeak through that with my teeth.

Like the previous three (or four) visits to the ER, Mom covered for me. Since she worked there and knew the staff, she was able to have them hide what I was taking so that way when I got spoken to from the hospital consoler, they would be left in the dark and I could talk my way out of it.

Now I know some of you are probably outraged by what I just wrote.

Angry even and asking "Why the fuck would she do that? Doesn't she want to help her son get better?"

And the answer to that is yes. Allow me to explain:

Had she not done that and forced me to go to shutter island I wouldn't be able to join the military, join the police force and face discrimination on every job interview I would get because I would have to check off 'yes' in the box asking if you have mental problems.

Get pissed at her all you want, but had she not done that, I don't know where I would be today. Probably not here writing this fucking book! She did a lot of things for me at this point, but the biggest thing she did was buy me time to get my head on straight.

She was also the one who found Ledner.

;

After being in his office for hours on end, Ledner prescribed three (or four) different meds at the same time. Two were for Bi-Polar and the other was an anti-seizer that also was known to help with mania in Bi-Polar patients. So at first, I thought I was in good shape. The side effects were 'tolerable' and the pills were small so they wouldn't be hard to swallow (that's what she said!).

Well, I hate to break it to you, but treating a mental illness isn't that fucking easy. If it was easy, then it wouldn't be an illness. Ledner described it as 'a shot in the dark' with no guarantee the meds would work right away or even at all. What would happen is if one or none of them worked, you would have to wean yourself off of each one and try a different another combination (sounds fun, right?).

Some fuckers are lucky and get their cocktail right the first time…others aren't so lucky.

And guess what?

That's right!

I WASN'T LUCKY!

My first round of drugs was ineffective to put it lightly. And I was fucking bullshit!

There I was, hoping and believing that once I hit the two-week mark for the meds to be in full effect, I was going to feel absolutely great and life would FINALLY go back to normal!

Nope.

I felt the fucking same.

I vividly remember becoming an absolute asshole during this time. I had struggled for weeks trying to get over the fact that I had to take medication after trying so hard not to and after all that the fucking pills didn't work.

I screamed, shouted, called and said things to those around me like I never had before. I made my mum cry, pissed off my stepdad and damn near anyone else who was close enough to hear me yell. And you can bet your ass the next time I saw Ledner, I ripped him a new asshole.

"Do you even know what the fuck you're doing? These fucking goddamn pills are fucking useless! Just like you. You make me wait out in the waiting room a half hour past our appointment every fucking time, you sit and stare at me like I'm some sort of goddamn criminal and then prescribe me shit that doesn't work! Are you really that much of a moron?!"

…

I'm paraphrasing (not by much, though) but trust me he knew I was fucking bullshit. Everyone else in the building did, too. Everyone stared at me when I walked out of his office, all with the same expression (guess I used my big boy voice when I told him he was fucking useless). I even brought up how fucking depressing all his dead planets were. I went scorched Earth on him!

But even after all that, Ledner never raised his voice, threw me out of his office or punched me. He just sat in his seat and remained civil. That pissed me off even more. It got to the point I asked him if he could prescribe me whatever the fuck he was on to stay calm.

After my little temper tantrum, Ledner reminded me that there were a bunch of medications to try out and to not give up so quickly. Easy for him to say, but I figured I wouldn't start up again.

He tacked on another pill that requires a medical license in order to pronounce it correctly. It was a relatively high dose, so he said it shouldn't take as long for it to set in. I was doubtful, but I just kept thinking about the patted room.

I took the prescription and made sure I followed his directions to ween off the ones that weren't working. He kept telling me to stop the medication slowly. I kept telling I would.

And I did.

At first.

By the end of the second day, I was tired of trying to figure out which pills were which, so I just stopped them all together and just stayed on the new ones. Yes, listening to your doctor is very important (I'm aware!), but what do you want me to lie to you and say I listen 100%? Sorry to disappoint.

Like the other fucking meds, the new ones didn't start right away either, which allowed time for me to focus on the fact that I wanted to tell Ledner to fuck off and go running to Tyler with open arms and say to him "I'm sorry I left, but it'll never happen again!".

But I didn't.

Though some days it was near impossible.

Looking back now, I'm actually surprised my knees didn't buckle (addiction is a heavy weight to carry). Deep down somewhere, I knew I was on the path to getting better, but I still felt alone (not to mention I knew the path was gonna a fucking long ass one too).

It's hard to explain (even now), but when you're going through all those feelings, urges and emotions, it takes a lot out of you and it gets to the point where you have no energy to go out, socialize or even talk to people. All you want to do is go home and jump in bed (just to stare at the fucking wall I might add).

Maybe you understand what that's like.

Maybe you don't.

I don't really give a shit, to be honest.

...

Sorry, that was kinda blunt; let me rephrase that:

Addiction doesn't just stop when you wake up one sunny morning and say "Oh jeez, I better stop doing drugs before I really cut my leg off next time." Admitting that is just the first step on this wonderful ride out of hell. Believe it or not boys and girls, there are two battles you go through with addiction: physically and then mentally.

There's no doubt about it: The mental battle is by far the worst fucking part about it.

Don't get me wrong, the physical battle is no picnic either. In fact, it's actually pretty fucking awful, but most of it happens in the beginning. Once you get past that (especially the first two or three weeks), then physically you're out of the doghouse, but it's that mental battle that fucks us up the most. Without question.

It's hard to ignore the voices in your head. I don't give a fuck who you are or what you say, no amount of medication can stop them and their evil ideas from popping up out of the darkest corners of your brain.

I knew the direction I was heading was a positive one, but it didn't feel any different from actually being at rock bottom; I could still feel the tips of the rocks poking at my ass cheeks. And it was obvious it would get harder before anything got easier.

10/6/2012

Its scary that it's close to a month since I last wrote in here and every thing else in between. Guess time really does take it all. All I can hope for is that one day I can get it all back. Maybe one, I'm hoping.

Yesterday made it month since the ER trip. But also the last time I used, so that's a good thing. Everyone keeps telling me 'small victory lead to large deafets'. Well see.

Not much has changed since last time. Im still taking the pills Ledner prescribed. Recently Ive been feeling better. I get very hungry though at night. I feel bad for yelling at Ledner before. Next time I see him Ill have to say sorry. Actually I see him next week.

Its been a month since everything, but it feels longer then that. Thinking about it makes me sad, but mum said it'll get better soon. Hoping so. I really miss her today. She slept downstairs last night. It was nice to have some company down here for once.

Getting ready for work. Trying to stay busy to keep my mind off things, so not sure when I'll get to write in this again. I'll try though.

Until next time ☺

;

The meds were working.

No other way to put it.

The contrast between this entry and the others is impossible to ignore, I actually smiled when I read it. The difference one page can make is simply amazing. Clearly, when I wrote that it was official:

MATT WAS BACK!

Yes, it took time and killed a piece of my soul that can never be healed, but finally, after a long a tough battle, the end of the fucking tunnel was not only in sight, but within reach. And as fun as the ride had been, I couldn't wait to fucking get off of it!

As I said before, there's a lot of details I'll never remember, but I remember around this time fairly well. Even now it's hard to put into words how it felt, but I guess the best way to describe it is like waking up one morning after a nasty ass cold. Your head isn't heavy, your body doesn't ache and most of all: your mind is clear.

That's how it felt.

It almost felt strange at first, because it was a feeling I hadn't felt in years (how fucking depressing is that?). But it was something else, to say the least. I didn't just pick up on it, either. One night around this time, I remember my mum coming down bawling her eyes out because even she saw a difference.

I felt proud. Call it whatever you want, but for me, it was a miracle during a time when I couldn't catch a break. Hell, some mornings I would wake up excited just because I got to take my pills (again, how fucking sad is that?).

Both mum and Ledner were afraid that I would have a hard time staying on them, which is I guess a common problem for us bipolar folk, but it turned out not to be. The first week or so was because I wasn't noticing a difference, but when I could start to feel a shift inside, I knew something, good or bad, was about to give way. And it turned out to be something good.

Lender still insisted that I see him once a week for a while (back when insurance was actually useful), which I didn't mind. Each time I was there, our sessions got shorter and shorter, so it was fine by me.

But even he was shocked by the results. Three weeks prior he said I was without a doubt, "one of the most difficult cases" of bipolar he'd seen in his twenty years of practicing (finally first place for something!).

I didn't count my chickens before they fucked, though. I was cautiously optimistic. Ledner was too, adding that if they did end up working, down the road at some point, they would have to be tweaked again to keep everything in line (there's that tolerance thing again!).

So basically what Ledner was saying was that he and I were going to know each other for a very long time. A month or two before this I would've told you that I'd rather eat shit than have to see him any more than I needed too, but since he clearly had steered me on the right track, I was willing to give him the benefit of the doubt.

But every cloud has a silver lining or some shit, and this was no exception. Ledner said that in order for me to stay on the medication, I was going to have to have blood work done more often than just once a year. It wasn't a big deal, so I said yes. He said I was gonna need to have it done every four months. I yelled at him.

Not long after, things were starting to settle down and I started feeling good. So good, that in fact, Ledner extended out our sessions from every week to every other week and at the peak of it all, to every month! I was shitting kittens because I was so happy!

Finally, light at the end of this fucking goddamn tunnel of misery was in my hands!

I was happy!

I was proud!

But I knew better.

I knew it was just a matter of time before the clog in the pipe dislodged and I would get sprayed in the face with shit again. Now, you can argue that I'm just being paranoid, and maybe there's logic to that, but I'd rather spend my life being prepared, then spend it trying to get over that one moment of being completely blindsided.

;

By early winter, I was back to 'normal' and had just gotten a new boss at work; Joey. I fucking hated him! He was loud, rude, mean and constantly on my ass over every little goddamn thing. He had just been promoted to manager and transferred to my store, so he was the 'fresh fish' for all of the other departments to shit on. I learned early on that he could handle himself, but despite me not really liking him at first, I worked my ass off and helped him fit in. It paid off because we ended up becoming really good friends.

He was an Italian born and raised in Massachusetts, so he had both the accent and the cockiness patted down to the max. At first, that's why I didn't really care for him, but as I got to know him, I quickly realized how cool he was. Funny as hell, too.

It was strange that he and I got along so well because we were the exact opposite: He was outgoing; I was a hermit. He was an arrogant ladies' man; I was a closet-case in love with a straight guy who I never had a shot with. He was good-looking, I made Quasimodo look like fucking Sinatra. I could go on and on, but we still hit it off.

Him and I worked side by side nearly every day. It became fun, but he was constantly on me, making sure I was doing shit right. That part about him sucked, but at the end of the day, he was still my boss and I was still just another slave worker getting paid shit. A lot changed when he and I started talking about our personal lives, though.

I remember it well.

The shitty grocery store chain we worked for had just opened up a new store down in Nashua, NH. The place was a fucking madhouse when it opened, and upper management reached out to managers of other stores and departments to help out. Of course, Joe got to be one of the lucky bastards forced into it, and since he was on salary, he wasn't getting paid a goddamn cent to go. Every goddamn day I had to listen to it.

He was told he was going to have to close down the department every night for about a week. He was told he could bring someone and as it just so happens, he decided to pick me!

Road trip!

Since Nashua was out of the way for both of us, we decided to carpool. One night he would drive, and the next, I would drive. Well, that's how it was supposed to go; he ended up conning me into driving most of the week. Of course, he did by us food, so maybe that evens out (if you want to call fast food actual food).

It was fun, to be honest. We worked, ate a bunch of free food the store offered because of the grand opening, and we got to boss the other workers around, so that was pretty fun. The only thing that really sucked ass was that we would get out late, and by the time I dropped him off at his car, it was going on midnight. But time went by fast, so I didn't mind.

I remember one night, (I think it was the last day we had to go, or pretty close to it), we got out REALLY fucking late. We were beyond exhausted, but we still carried on our rather inappropriate conversations. They were hilarious, though; not gonna lie about that.

Joey—trying to be the ladies' man that he was—had been attempting to date this chick that worked up front for months, but was getting nowhere, and he was pissed about it! "I've been with a dozen girls, and none of them made me have to work this hard to get their attention."

"Maybe she doesn't like you?" I asked, stating the obvious.

He scoffed. "Come on, Matty. How could you not like this?"

"Maybe you should ask her and find out."

"Fuck you!" I remember him hitting me in the arm.

He kept saying that he was gonna ride it out because he really wanted to get with her. I tried to make him feel better, but like always, he called my bluff. But then the conversation shifted to me.

"What about you, Matty? You got a girl?"

I'm a firm believer that work should stay at work and home should stay at home. I looked at Joe as a friend, but at the end of the day, he was still my boss and could fire my ass at a moment's notice. I chose not to tell him I'm into cock, but I was honest on another front.

"No, I got a lot of shit I'm going, though. Last thing I need is to complicate it with a relationship."

Being the shit that he was, Joe kept asking for more details. Over and over, it was obvious he wasn't going to shut the fuck up until I said something, and we were still a long way from home.

"I'm an addict," I shouted out loud.

Joe got silent. "Really?"

"Yeah."

"You don't look like one."

"No, I'm not now, but I mean I was."

"Oh...sorry to hear that. How you holding up?"

I was honest. "Not too bad, actually. Been feeling pretty good lately. Course you always have me working like a dog, so I don't get much time by myself."

"Shit, dude. I'm sorry."

"Don't be. Staying busy is a good thing."

He patted me on the shoulder. "Well, if you need anything, let me know. I've been through this before with one of my buddies from college, so I have experience with this."

His words meant a lot, almost ringing what Tyler would say to me when I was going through shit. It's fucking amazing what the smallest things do for people (unless you're referring to a micropenis, then you're kinda screwed).

"Thanks, Joe."

"No problem, but if I find out you're back on stuff, I'll kick your fucking ass! I mean it."

I chuckled. "Okay."

Looking back now, it's clear that was the night when we went from work friends to actual friends. Hell, I even told him that I was sorry for thinking he was an asshole when I first met him.

Aside from getting pulled over because I ran a red light, the rest of the ride home was kind of nice. I actually felt sad that we weren't gonna be doing the road trips anymore, but that night must've stayed with him too because from that point on, I only worked when he was working.

Good times.

Great times!

And still friends to this very day.

No, he never got together with that chick.

He still bitches about that, to this very day, too.

12/31/2012

8:43

Goodbye 2012!

No doubt this has been one of the worst years I've been through. It's amazing how much can change in just 12 months. Never really thought of it before, but I do now. Time flies when you take your eyes off the clock.

Not everything was bad though. There's been a couple good times and even some laughs. I'm hoping there's alittle more next year, but at this point Ill take what I can get.

Still taking the meds and feeling good so maybe that's a good way to start the new year. Don't have high expectations for 2013 but anything will be better than this year. Gonna try and stay positive. Maybe itll work.

I still get urges sometimes. Mostly at night. Haven't acted on them and don't think I will. It actually feels good to feel normal for once and I don't want to screw it up so im going to try not to.

I guess this is when your supposed to make a list of what you want next year to be like. So here it goes

1:better than 2012
2:stay away from drugs
3:fall in love
4:stay in love
5:write a book
6:be happy
7:be me

I'm probably asking for to much, but its always good to aim high I guess. Besides I'll be willing to take even just one of those things. Gonna work to get them all though!

I haven't thought about suicide for a while. Maybe that means #6 is already being worked on. Guess I'll find out next year.

So goodbye 2012
Hello 2013

;

I woke up to the smell of vomit. I must've smelled it at some point during the night, but slept through it anyway. But once my bloodshot eyes opened for the morning, there wasn't a chance in hell that I could've ignored it. It took a bit for my eyes to adjust to the overhead lights, but once they did, and I got my glasses on, I rejoined reality.

Projectile vomit was sprayed not just across my bed, but all over my pillow and up the walls, and I couldn't remember a fucking thing. NOT ONE THING.

The purplish puke smelt worse than a rotting corpse, but somehow, someway, I was able to sleep through it anyway (skill right there). Waking up to a mystery is always a little nerve-racking, but I'd done it a hundred times before, so it wasn't anything new for me. I just needed to figure out what the fuck happened. It somewhat started coming together when I got out of my puke covered bed and found an empty bottle of spiced rum on the floor. But before I could start playing detective, I needed to do something about the mess I had.

Everyone in the house was sleeping, which allowed me to throw out my sheets in the trashcans outside, and open up the windows and back door to the basement to get the fucking smell out.

I still had a mattress full of food and stomach acid I needed to clean up too, but first I wanted to see if I could scrape together any memories from the night before. I was stumped at first. I knew there wasn't any 'illegal' pills in the house and I wouldn't have taken any of mum's medication because she was home (not to mention she fucking locked them all up).

...

I was lost.

Confused.

And had a really bad stomach ache.

I checked my body for any signs of blood or cuts, (or attempted amputations) and found nothing, which was good, but it only added to the mystery. At least if there was blood, I'd have something to go on, but I didn't. All I had was an empty liquor bottle, and a bed full of my previous meal (which wasn't even decipherable).

I had woken up to many 'mysteries' over the years, but this one took the cake. I had not one fucking clue as to what in the Christ happened. I was so dumbfounded, that I actually gave some thought to going upstairs and asking anyone in the house if they could help me out, or point me in the right direction. But since I had clearly done a bit of drinking, and was still under that magical age of 21, I decided to ax that idea.

After giving it some serious thought, and trying to piece together something (anything) that made sense, I decided I would ignore the entire situation and pretend that it never happened!

I would clean up the vomit, scrub the walls, buy new bedsheets, promise myself to never drink again and simply move on with life. Easy as that, right?

At first, it was.

I actually got through most of the day without really giving it any thought. Toward the evening, I thought I was in the clear, proving to myself that it was just another one of those glitches that come along in life. I figured since I was confident that I didn't relapse on any pills, it was okay.

But like almost every other thing in this fucking story, it all shifted at night.

I didn't have to work New Year's day, so I spent the day at home. I stayed in my windowless basement for basically the whole day. Since I didn't have a smartphone way back in the day, if you wanna call 2013 back in the day, I had to go on an actual computer to check my social media, and right before I planned on going to bed I did. That was when I found that one big piece of the puzzle I'd been missing.

When I got to the post on my screen, I read it over and over, making sure my eyes weren't fucking around on me like they'd done so many times before. My chest started heaving when I was sure. Followed soon after by sadness.

Posted by one of my friends back in high school was:

'Gone to soon, rest easy Tyler...'

...

...

...

I wasn't sure how to react. I didn't react at first. I stayed neutral.

It took me some time to figure out how I wanted to respond. Probably a lot longer than it should've, but as I reread the post, I realized that it was posted two days prior. That's when I knew it wasn't the first time I saw it. And that was also when I understood what had happened to me the night before.

The picture that was attached to the post was clearly a much older picture, probably meaning there wasn't a more recent photo of him, which in that and of itself is depressing enough. He did look happy, though. It was nice to see proof that he smiled sometimes, or at least at one point in his life.

No matter how hard I tried to think back though, I couldn't, and still can't, remember the last time I saw him or the last time we talked. I know more than likely it was probably the last time I bought drugs from him, but the part that has always bothered me is that when I would go to see him, it was never just about drugs. We would shoot the shit, make each other laugh, and even get shit off our chest; shit that we never mentioned to anybody else. Hell, that was one of the reasons why I always enjoyed buying drugs from him.

Since I deleted his number out of my phone last time I got shipped to the ER, there was no way for me to talk to him. We simply split apart without any real type of closure. And there's nothing worse than holding onto a goodbye that you'll never get to say, trust me.

Like I said before, you can think of Tyler however you want, but he never has, and never will be, the villain in my book. I was the villain.

I was the antagonist.

I was the one that fucked everything up.

Not him.

So if you wanna be pissed at someone, be pissed at me, I can take it.

I may not remember the last time we spoke, but I do remember one of the moments we had during the early days of our friendship.

"What would your dream job be?" Tyler once asked me during one of our deals.

"A writer."

"Why?"

"Always thought I had a story to tell."

"So what're you doing, here?"

;

More than likely it was a drug overdose that did it. I never asked, or even really wanted to know to tell you the truth, but it's hard to ignore the writing on the wall. I gave serious thought to going to the service, but in the end, I decided not to. I should've, but I was afraid that those old familiar feelings were going to come along for the ride. Not to mention it would've felt a little strange going, since I was someone who bought drugs from him. Something like that is kind of hard to explain to a grieving family.

I didn't get drunk again that night (I was out of booze), but I did take the time to look back and replay all those moments from gym class to our obnoxious text messages we would send each other. It wasn't a normal friendship in any sense, but it was still a friendship. It was hard to say goodbye, but the sun always sets. That night, January 1st, 2013 was no different.

2013 clearly made one hell of an entrance, as I struggled not to head to the exit.

;

"I'm sorry to hear that about your friend," Ledner said in his usual flat-toned voice.

"Thanks. I'm gonna miss him," I said questioning why I even brought Tyler up to him, when I just wanted to leave his dead planet filled office.

"You met in school?"

"Ya."

"You were close?"

"Sorta."

"Fascinating…" Ledner kept saying as he wrote everything down. "You would…chill after school?"

"Not really, I would just buy drugs from him and go home."

I kicked myself even as the words came out because I fucking knew Ledner was going to start asking questions and my half hour appointment was about to be doubled. And sure enough, that's exactly what fucking happened.

"Oh, dear…"

I rolled my eyes as I stared at the clock, wishing I could somehow make time go by faster.

"Well, that is concerning," Ledner started. "When was the last time you saw this Tyler character?"

"Can't remember."

"Huh…" Ledner clearly didn't believe me. "Okay…and what types of drugs would you get from him exactly?"

"You a cop?"

By the look on Ledner's face, he clearly wasn't expecting my response. "No…I'm just trying to get a sense of your friendship, so I can figure out how you're probably feeling."

"He's dead. What's there to feel about?"

Ledner kept on writing. "Well, just because someone is dead, doesn't mean we stop caring about them."

No argument there. In fact, Ledner had a totally solid point. It was annoying every time he would ask about my feelings while he treated me like a fucking lab rat, but sometimes the guy made sense and even gave off the cold illusion that somewhere deep down, he might not be an emotionless robot every day of his life.

"So aside from your drug dealer's death, how're you feeling?"

"Fine."

"How's work?"

"Fine."

"How's the home life?"

"Fine."

"How's everything else?"

"Take one fricken guess."

"Fine?"

I made sure he saw me roll my eyes. "Really?"

"You said guess," Ledner said as he kept on writing every word I said down. "And medication wise, how're you feeling? Anything you feel needs to be tweaked or in need of a refill?"

I shrugged. "No, I think I'm good."

Basically, every answer I gave Ledner on this particular day was short because I just wanted to get the fuck out of that office, and the answer to his last question didn't need to be any longer.

The fact was aside from Tyler's death and a few bumps in the road with my straight 'boyfriend', things were a lot better off than they were even a year before. I couldn't deny that.

"Good…" Ledner said before giving his final take on everything.

I did what I would normally do near the end of our little sessions, I completely blocked him out. I don't remember exactly what he said, but it went something along the lines of he thought I was doing well, I was going to be a little sad because of Tyler, but I would eventually move on, and he wrote me some refills in case I needed something.

He also reminded me that life isn't always perfect. In fact, it normally never is. Every day can't be good, but it can be managed, well most could anyway he added. I paid attention to that part since he was actually making sense.

It was true: life wasn't perfect at that moment, but it wasn't horrible either. It was level.

Being level may not be the most exciting way to live life, but it was something I could adjust to, and even live with.

I got used to that idea, fast.

7/7/2014

Wow! How fast does time fly!

It doesn't feel like a year and a half at all. Time really does go by faster the older you get. Maybe grandpa was right.

A lot has happened since last time. Some good and some bad, but overall I've had worse, that's for sure.

Drug free for almost 2 years now!

Ran into some problems with my meds a while back. Got alittle scary or a second, but doing what I gotta do. On 6 or 7 meds now. Proves how messed up I am I guess!

Last year Ledner diagnosed me with 'Rapid Cycle Bi Polar'. That was a tough day. Least now its starting to make sense and now I know why my father was such an asshole. Scared I'll be like him though.

Starting a new job tomorrow. Kinda nervous because it's a real job now, but sounds like the money will be good. Hopefully before the year is up I'll save up enough for a new car. Gonna miss Joey, though.

Still single, but I knew that would happen. Doubt that'll change this year, but maybe next year will be the year. Joe keep telling me to keep lookin, but its not that easy.

;

Without a doubt, one of the more larger gaps in the journal, but not on purpose; I just think over time I started focusing on other things and before you know it, one week turns to one month and then one month turns to one year. The first sentence says it all though:

TIME REALLY DOES FUCKING FLY!

Remember that ladies and gents!

Picking up where we left off back in 2013, the first half of the year was not much better than the beauty that was 2012. In fact, it was shaping up to be the exact same fucking thing! It took some time for the tide to shift.

I chose not to go to Tyler's wake. Instead I 'signed' the guest book on the funeral website, did my best to face reality and move on. It wasn't easy, but it wasn't like I had a choice.

At the beginning of the year, Ledner and I saw each other about every other week, but that started to stretch the further we got into 2014 because the meds were working so good. 2013, however, was a different story to say the fucking least. At that point, I was still on five different meds (I believe), which may sound like a lot to those pricks, not on any prescription medication, but it's not exactly a bad thing. Allow me to explain:

Let's say instead of being on those 5 pills, Ledner just put me on one.

Would it work? No guarantee, but yes it could (and probably would).

So now you're thinking: "Well if just one goddamn pill would work, why does your strange-ass therapist have you on five of them?"

GREAT QUESTION!

And the answer is simple: SIDE EFFECTS!

Yes, my fellow readers, that's the short and sweet answer. Here's why:

If Ledner had put me on only one type of med, the dose would need to be relatively high so it would be effective. Makes sense, right?

BUT the higher the dose, the more likely it is that you start to really feel the side effects. And trust me when I say mental health prescription side effects are not something you want to deal with! They range from hair loss to a fucking limp dick, and I don't know about you, but I don't really want to be on Viagra before I'm fucking 30. No thank you! I'd rather risk a mental breakdown and life in the padded room than take boner pills any day of the week.

I knew that. Ledner knew that.

This is where the other meds come in:

If you can come up with a combination of different medications that still treat your condition, then the multiple pills can offset the high dosage you would need if you were just on one pill. So rather than being on one high dosage, you go on multiple dosages that are small, thus decreasing many of those beautiful side effects.

This is called a 'cocktail'.

This is without a doubt the most important part of treating any type of mental disorder. It's also the most painstaking. It can really be difficult to get it right, and if it's not right, you'll never get better. It's that black and white. There is no such thing as gray area when it comes to this.

The beginning half of 2013 was tough because we had to start over even though as great as the meds were working, I told Ledner I needed to get off one because of the side effects.

I had gained over 50 pounds because of this one medication I was on that was known to cause weight gain. Once I took a look in the mirror and took a good look at the man boobs and double chin that was starting to form, I went right to him and said: "take me off these damn things and let's try something else".

It seems like a fairly simple thing to do, right? Just ween yourself off and start something new. Sounds pretty simple.

Guess what? It's fucking not.

Ledner insisted that I really think about if I wanted to get off them because he warned that it would drastically change my mood until we found a replacement. At this point, I'd known Ledner for about two years. He has no sense of humor, no type of emotion and probably no feelings (could be wrong), but the fact that he took the time to warn me beforehand really forced me to give it a second thought.

But against his better judgment, I chose to shake things up. I could tell he was two steps away from rolling his eyes, but he went with it and we spent the rest of the session looking for new meds.

;

The first few days were fine; in fact, I didn't notice a difference. This time I made sure to follow the instructions of weaning myself off, because of how much higher the dosage was on these ones. I held my own and kept positive... until about day four. Then I started to feel things beginning to shift.

Yes, I was still taking the other pills he prescribed me, but I had to carefully start the new one while carefully weaning myself off the other (basically a balancing act). But I get impatient fast, and guess what? I started to get impatient fast.

The goal was to make sure the new pill slowly offset the other pill, but halfway through, I said the hell with it and stopped the old one altogether, fucking up the balance and causing that shift Ledner had warned about. And before I knew it, those feelings were right there, ready to greet me back.

When you have Bipolar, you're either extremely happy/mad or extremely sad/depressed. Most time I would fall on the sad side—which is why Ledner first diagnosed me with Bi-Polar II, but this time was a bit of a changeup. This time I landed on the mad side.

For well over a week, I was a complete fucking asshole! I was loud, rude and yelled damn near every day. It got so bad that Joey had to send me home one day after I told a customer to go fuck themselves. It was even worse when I was home.

I must've made my mum cry every other day. I was such a dick to her and said things that even to this day, I regret. It was strange; one second I was yelling and screaming, and then the next I was coming back upstairs all misty-eyed saying I was sorry.

I knew she was hurt by the things I said, but she always forgave me and kept insisting that she would keep an eye on me. And she did, and I would yell. All of that only lasted about a week, but it felt like an eternity. Towards the end, it was scary, because every once in a while, if it was quiet enough, I could feel those argues approaching.

Then, FINALLY after week two, I started feeling like my normal self again. Great news! The side effects of the new med weren't nearly as bad or had as many as some of the others, but one of the most common was drowsiness/tiredness.

Now, I've been very tired before and had to crawl my way through a day, but that fucking medication brought it to a whole new level that I didn't think was possible.

Before the med change, I would be up and about by 7:00 am. After I started taking it, I'd be lucky if I was up by noon. And when I would get up, it would take at least a half hour for me to be awake enough to find the energy to stand. One morning I was so knocked out, mum came downstairs and actually checked my pulse to make sure I wasn't dead.

They worked well, even better than the other pills, but man did they hit you hard once they set in. I found out after reading online that they've actually be used as a date rape drug. Lucky me! But at least that would mean I'd have a tolerance so any rapist would need to use a lot more on me (there's those small victories again!).

Actually, for a while there, they were pretty hard to handle. It took a lot of energy to force myself up after taking them the night before, let alone try and shake it off before the rest of the day started. It was like a hangover that would never go away, no matter how much coffee or energy drinks you gulped down.

Did they work?

Yes.

Problem was, they were only working because I spent the whole day trying not to fall back asleep. It was like walking around as a fucking zombie, and not one of the ones nowadays that actually run after you, I'm talking fucking old school zombie that moves two feet in four hours. That's how bad it was, and Ledner wanted the dose to be higher.

HIGHER!

"You trying to turn me into a fucking vegetable?" I remember asking him when he bumped up the strength another couple hundred milligrams.

After telling me, yet again, that he doesn't care for the language, he explained to me that it takes time for the body to adjust to the medication, but it'll get better once everything is tweaked right.

I wasn't happy, but I listened and I kept taking the damn things.

But boy was Ledner right!

It took some fucking time, that's for sure!

Especially after that last bump up in strength. It got to the point where I completely forgot what happens in the world during the morning. My morning was the afternoon, or just before, if I was lucky.

This was around the time when I started drinking black coffee. It tasted like engine oil, but every day on my way to work, I would buy it and down it quick as I could. Sometimes, especially when I first started, it took the edge off, but not always. I'm telling you, those fucking pills could knock a fucking goddamn horse on its ass. They were terrible!

I resisted and I fought every day that desire to just give up…but I didn't. I just kept listening to mum every time I would start bitching.

"It'll get better."

"It'll get better."

"It'll get better."

Somedays I wanted to throw something at her for sounding like a broken record, but I just kept doing what I could in order to get past the fact that I felt like I was dying a little inside with each passing day.

It was a long battle to get back to stable ground, and I kept kicking myself in the ass for deciding to shake things up when shit had just calmed down.

;

I thought nothing of it then, but now after giving it thought, it's clear that Joe saw my struggle, too.

"You're doing good, keep this shit up and you'll be promoted to manager," he said to me one day after I worked with him side by side in the back room.

He always knew what to say to get a smile on my face, but it had very little effect. The meds were really getting the best of me, and even I noticed a real slow down with my pace in the final weeks. He was patient, though.

But even with Joe's support, it was still my battle to get through myself. Support is nice, but in the end its still you that has to chug up the hill. It was a slug out that just seemed to go on and on.

After reaching the two-week mark and passing it, I did notice a bit of a difference; I wasn't as tired and groggy, but that wasn't saying much. I was still half past dead in the morning.

I can't deny that they worked, though. No matter how much I bitch about them. I could feel them working (when I was actually awake), and it felt like the plane was finally stabilizing again. It only took a fucking goddamn month from my life that I'll never get back, but hey, progress is progress. And to my amazement, things appeared to get better.

Ledner was happy with the results.

Mum was happy with the results.

And everyone else was happy with the results.

...

So it this it?

Is this where we finally get closure?

That happily, ever after?

FINALLY????

Does this goddamn pisser of a story end here?

Yes, it does.

Everything turned out great, I live a wonderful life and look back with fond memories!

Thank you for reading this!

Have a great day and wonderful life!

Just kidding!

7/10/2014

Absolutly horrible day. Just started the new job at the Billing Department. I have no idea what I'm doing and there's so much work. I don't want to go back. I really thought about just leaving for lunch and never going back.

Im gonna fuck stuff up and then Ill get fired and this will all be for nothing. Mum kept telling me all day to just take it slow. I cant do it.

Working with Joe on Sunday so maybe he can help. I feel lost.

Its days like this where no amount of medication in the world will help.

;

I was a recovering addict.

Bipolar was kicking my ass.

I was fucking a straight guy.

My self-esteem was shot.

My social life was nonexistent.

And I lost any confidence in myself years back.

That's where I was when I started that new job. And that's attempting to look on the bright side.

Working with Joe was great, but no full-time positions were open and I desperately needed a new car. The piece of shit Oldsmobile wasn't going to pass inspection in any way, shape, or form. Basically, I was fucked, to put it simply.

The money I had saved up between then and my last birthday was nothing short of a joke. I had barely two cents to my name. Joe did every single thing he could to get me as many hours as possible, but when (then) President Obama signed this thing where no part-timer can work more than 30-35 hours, it was a kick to the balls.

Every Sunday, Joe would have me work an 8-hour shift and close down the department. Many of the other part-timers in the department were always pissed because I was the one who only got the 8 hours and Sundays were 'time and a half'. He didn't care though, he kept giving them to me every week. But after Obama's order, I lost that, too.

"I'm sorry, Matty," I remember him saying to me.

It was then when I knew I was gonna have to move on, and I ended up telling him that. I figured I'd get the whole 'Matty, you can't leave me! Your mine forever, you son of a bitch!', but to my astonishment, it was the exact opposite. Not only did he understand, but he also said that he'd help me if I needed anything.

And like always, he was true to his word.

A few months after I had an interview, the company called him up and he did his thing: he dazzled them with bullshit. I was next to him when he got the call and he purposely made sure that I couldn't hear him talking, which only added to the tension.

Finally, after what must've been a solid half hour, he came back over with a large grin on his face.

"So, how'd it go?"

He patted me on the shoulder and smiled. "Oh, Matty. I'm sorry, but I had to tell them everything. I mean I couldn't lie. And now that I told them everything, I don't think they'll be calling back."

I was confused, borderline teary-eyed.

The look on Joey's face was serious and emotionless. It sent chills down my spine. I started to panic as my heart sank to my fucking shoes.

"What?" I asked all misty-eyed.

He walked over to me, patted me on the shoulder and took a deep breath. "I know this is gonna be hard to hear...but I can't let you go. You're too important here and I'm not in a position for you to leave just yet. I have to look out for me, you know?"

I was bullshit.

FUCKING BULLSHIT!

Joey just watched as I screamed, shouted, called him every name in the book and kept telling him to go fuck himself. And I only got angrier when he started laughing.

"What's so fucking funny?"

Joey caved. "I'm kidding shithead. You really think I would've done that to you?"

I punched him in the arm before thanking him. "Asshole."

"Love you too, Matty. Let me know what they say."

I knew Joe had done me a huge favor, but I wouldn't know just how big until much further down the road.

I was nervous, though. I didn't hear anything for months. After the second month, I assumed I didn't get it. Even Joe said I should've heard back by that point.

So I moved on.

I was mad that I didn't even get a fucking phone call, but still, I went back to the drawing board and started the job search again. During that time, I must've applied to a dozen different places. Everything from a mailman to a fucking waste management worker. I was desperate.

DESPERATE!

...

Then finally, almost four months after Joe got the call, I heard back from the Billing Department

I got the job.

I flipped the fuck out!

I was so excited. $14 an hour, paid time off, flexible work hours; I had hit the mother load.

Mum was happy.

Joe was happy.

Even Ledner was happy.

I started training a few days before my birthday, but I was upbeat...until I realized one little tiny thing.

"Joe," I said during my last week.

"What?"

"I just realized...I have no idea what the new job is."

"What? You must've read the description before applying."

"Ya, but it's been so fucking long, I don't remember what the description was."

After laughing his ass off, Joe said I would be fine but warned me that he was planning on working me to death until my last day. But I didn't care; hell, half the time it didn't even feel like work anyway and that last week was no different.

Great Example:

On my last day, Joe made me work-five hours in the morning so I could help him unload the produce truck and get the place ready to go for our wonderful food stamp customers.

Now in all fairness, I had every intention of working my ass off to make sure Joe was set before I left, but to our surprise, one of the co-workers in the back brought in jello shots for me because she knew how much I liked them.

"Jesus, how many are there?" I asked.

"Twenty," she said with a smile.

"WHAT?" Joe shouted. "What the hell is Matt gonna do with twenty jello shots? He gets drunk after two!"

I chose to leave them in the back room and would pick them up before I left, but like always, things changed.

"You know Matty...if you were a friend, you'd let me have a jello shot," Joey said with a smile.

"Course you can!" I said, what the fuck was I going to do with twenty jello shots, anyway?

We walked out back into the cut fruit room, and Joe took them out of the refrigerator. "What're you doing?"

"Having a jello shot."

"What? We're working."

"It's just one, it's not going to hurt anything. You can have one, with me."

I know you're judging me right now, but how the fuck could I pass up a jello shot from my boss? It's not as easy as you think! Besides, it was only one and it was small.

So, at seven in the morning while being punched in for work, we each took one, and holy shit was it strong! I could feel my liver being chewed away. Even Joe was taken off guard by how strong the damn thing was. We did get a burst of energy, though so there's one positive way to look at it.

But it wasn't long before the other guys in the department found out about the shots and wanted to join in. So they did.

At the start of the morning, there were twenty jello shots

At the start of the afternoon, there were eight.

And you should've seen it.

It was beautiful.

With the exception of one or two of the workers in the back, we were all plastered. Every time one of us would head in the back, we'd cut through the cut fruit room and take a shot. Every single one of us did.

Joe had at least four.

The rest of the guys must've had three each.

And I must've had at least three.

The store manager had been on vacation for the week, so no one in upper management came over to the department. Thank God for that because all of us would've ended up getting fired.

It was a great way to leave, but my day didn't end at noon like I thought it was going to.

"I'm heading home, Joe," I said with a bit of a slur.

"No, come here," he said with a bit of a slur himself.

I walked right up to him and he shined a flashlight in my eye. "You're drunk."

"Am not."

"Your eyes are fucking bloodshot! I can't let you go home like this."

"What the hell am I supposed to do, then?"

Joe shrugged. "I'll have you work an eight-hour shift so you can sober up, alright?"

"Sure!"

That's right, I stayed at work for an eight-hour shift so I could sober up before going home. How fucking cool is that? Even now, I'm laughing my ass off.

Joe and I had been in a number of situations that could've been used as a comedy sketch, but none of them could ever come close to topping that. I look back at that with fond memories.

Between noon and the time we left, both he and I must've drunk three coffees to stay awake. Joe's poker face could earn him an Emmy nomination, but I folded like a royal flush.

It was a long, unproductive, day you could say, but we both made it. As soon as it was 5:00, we both gunned it to clock out as fast as we could before a customer stopped and asked us to help them out.

But we made it out in one piece. By the time we got to our cars, we had sobered up just enough to be able to get home, but before we did, we had to say goodbye.

"You're gonna do fine, Matty. You work anything like you do here, you'll be on your way to CEO."

"I'm gonna miss you, Joe."

We hugged.

It was a long hug.

A loooooooooooong hug.

"Okay…" Joe said.

We both laughed. "Thank you, Joe."

"Stay in touch, asshole. Don't make me call your mother."

"I will."

"Alright, later Matty."

"Bye, Joe."

The ride home felt long, but I was fine with that. It gave me the chance to go back and relive all the stupid, outrageous, fun shit we got to do together over the years.

Yes, it was work, but I'd be lying if I said it wasn't some of the funniest moments in my life. I got to meet some great people, do some stupid things, eat tons of free food and got paid to do it all!

As I made my way down the highway, and toward my house, I felt proud, happy, and even hopeful. It was almost like I could feel myself slowly starting to build the life I wanted (or at the very least, setting up the foundation). It was a great feeling, a feeling that not even the strongest narcotics can provide, though they do come close to be fair.

I rode down the highway, in that piece of shit rusted out Oldsmobile, with a smile on my face and an eye on the future, hoping for the best, all the while completely ignoring the fact that I hadn't taken any of my medications for over six months.

9/2014

Lost.

;

This entry didn't have a complete date like the others, but one can assume it wasn't long after the previous one. And the entry itself speaks volumes anyway (give or take).

;

Every story has a twist you never see coming and guess what? The previous page was my twist you never saw coming.

That's right, between that large gap in the entries, somewhere along the way I had stopped all my medications completely.

EVERY

SINGLE

FUCKING

ONE

OF

THEM!

Now I'm sure you're probably rolling your eyes because of my stupidity, and you were hoping this fucking story would just end already so you can get on with whatever life awaits you outside of these pages (I feel your pain, trust me), but for those select few who are still here and asking why the fuck I would do something like that, allow me to answer that for you:

You ready?

…

You sure?

…

Okay here it is:

The reason why I stopped everything was because (drum roll), everything was okay.

I'm sure I lost some of you, so I'll rephrase that: At the height of my 'stabilization', (let's call it) I felt like I could rule the world if given the chance (and the right amount of caffeinated beverage). I had energy, confidence and actually started enjoying life with no sad feelings or suicidal thoughts in sight. Basically, I'm saying at this point I stopped wishing I was too stubborn to die.

Life was good.

I had made it.

I survived.

...

So since I felt so good, then there's no need to keep taking my pills, right?

...

I've made some dumb choices and mistakes in my life, but this one was, without a doubt, one of the dumbest fucking ones. Like every other time in my life, when things got stable, I had to roll a grenade into the picture. Probably the best way to describe it is, like a pilot reaching 35,000 feet and he decides to leave the cockpit to take a nap in the back since everything is going so smooth.

Looking in the rearview mirror, I wish I could find a way to travel back in time, grab the younger version of me by the neck, and tell him to open his fucking eyes and read the warning signs!

But I can't.

After I stabilized, I got cocky, careless and took the situation for granted when Ledner and everyone else warned me to keep my guard up.

I didn't keep my guard up.

The younger version of me did ignore the warning signs.

And I set myself up on yet again another unnecessary collision course.

;

While I don't exactly remember when I stopped, I do remember feeling fine after I did. Ledner had warned me for years that a sudden stop in anything would be 'disastrous'. I knew he said that, but I think—despite everything I had gone through—I was still holding out hope that maybe he got it wrong and all I needed was a little push in the right direction. I even started questioning my bipolar diagnosis.

I remember starting to believe that clear as day, a perfect example of how much of a fucking idiot I was.

Sitting here in this dimly lit room, I can't help but think a part of me was still in denial, or still just as foolish as I had been years back, or maybe a mix of both. Who the hell knows.

All I can say is that, after I started feeling normal (if there is such a thing), I decided I was cured, I could leave my meds behind and focus on the rest of my life. And that's what I did.

At first, I couldn't help but hear Ledners warning echoing over and over in my head, but I was still confident that I was fixed. To be on the safe side,

I did keep my guard up in case I started feeling like I was heading toward that familiar rabbit hole.

But I didn't fall into the rabbit hole.

I didn't feel sad, or angry, or mad, or depressed.

I felt like me.

There was no sudden shift, angry outburst, or sudden relapse in suicidal tendencies. Everything remained stable, to my astonishment. I was pleasantly surprised for once.

I started questioning Ledners judgment because his 'warnings' seemed to be just empty words. I could've chosen to get pissed again and shout at him, but I focused on the whole idea that I didn't need medication anymore.

It might sound fucked up to someone like yourself, but I was so proud of myself. For the first time in years, I felt like I had stumbled across a fucking miracle, and I couldn't have been happier. The feeling didn't stop either. I went months with no medication at all and I felt great. In fact, so much time passed, I nearly forgot about the medication altogether.

But I wouldn't learn until later how serious what I was doing would end up being.

;

For those of you who don't know much about mental illness (lucky fucks) allow me to share a small piece of information with you: this might come as a surprise, but sometimes the people who are on meds don't really want to take them.

"But why not?" you're probably thinking. "Why wouldn't you want to take something that makes you feel better? I mean honestly, how hard is it to swallow a goddamn fucking pill you fudge packer?"

Again, there's a solid argument in there because you're right, it's not difficult to take a pill (or seven), every day, but it's hard to keep taking them when you feel like nothing's wrong.

Ask yourself why would you continue taking Viagra if you feel like you don't have a problem getting a hard on?

That's how I felt.

And that's why I stopped.

You don't need what you don't have, right?

Like I said, looking back, it was a massive fuck up on my part, but life was okay then. Work was going fine with Joe, I was rebuilding bridges at home, and I was getting laid on a regular basis. What more could you ask for?

It stayed that way too, which is why it was so goddamn easy to leave them behind. So between that, and Ledner extending our sessions out so long, it was the perfect opportunity to allow myself to stay unchecked.

But, like always, nothing lasts forever.

This situation is no fucking different.

And when we flash forward to the first week at the new job, that was where things started shifting.

;

The first week of the new job was awful, and the weeks and months that followed were no better. I felt like I was surrounded by people who knew everything there was to know about insurance companies and how their billing operations work, and there I was, stuck in a windowless room, completely lost, with no sense of direction at all.

Like every place you work at, there are some very nice people, and there are some cock-smooching assholes. The Billing Department was no different. The very nice people were awesome; they helped me and tried to guide me in the right direction every time I had a question or problem, and there were many. So, on that front, the job was okay.

But those cock-smooching assholes get their name for a reason. Since I was surrounded by only women, a lot of cage rattling happened for no particular reason. Some of the cock-smooching assholes I was able to keep at bay; I just smiled at them and said thank you for showing me where I fucked up. The others, though...not so much.

There's always that one person who is so much a cock-smooching asshole, they drag everyone down, and boy did I have one of those. Supposedly, outside of work, she was great and fun to be around, but she was a pure bitch to work with (I'd say a different word, but I'm gonna take the high road).

I don't know what it was I did, but she hated me (probably still does), and that bugged me because I always went out of my way to try and get along with everyone, and I did get along with everyone, except her. She was about as friendly as the North Korean dictator.

So between that and the fact that I had no fucking idea what I was doing and worried I was going to get fired, was the reason why that stabilization came crashing down. Pretty quickly, too.

That's when those all too familiar feelings emerged from the shadows once again.

;

Nearly all of my prescriptions were empty, and all of the refills had expired. I was on my own, again, with nothing but my thoughts carrying me back to that evil place I thought I'd left behind (or thought I did). It wasn't until that moment when I realized you can't run from your past. All you can do is hope that when you fall back down the rabbit hole, it isn't as deep as before.

I called Ledner first. I had no intention of telling him that I stopped all my medication; my plan was to just ask him for more refills. That plan shit the bed when I called and his fucking thousand-year-old secretary said he was on vacation for two weeks. I knew right then and there that I was completely fucked, and not in a good way, either.

Remember that conversation we had a bunch of pages back, where I attempted to explain to you normal people about how it takes a few weeks for meds to really kick in? Well, it was bad enough that I knew I was going to have to find a way to make it through two weeks, but now I was facing an entire fucking month. AT LEAST!

Yes, I was older and much wiser than I was years back, but depression is depression no matter how much lipstick you put on it. The first few days were bad, but I knew the worst was still on the horizon.

The home life was fine, but my attitude changed that. I would come home either pissed or depressed (normally depressed) and would end up getting into shouting arguments with mum. I thought about telling her but stopped short fearing that this would be the final straw that would ship me off to the padded room. I made a lot of progress since the last ER visit, but the bridge was still damaged.

And last, but not least: the love life.

The horrible, shitty, depressing, beautiful, love life.

That was in the shitter, too. But that's what happens when you're secretly with a straight guy; sometimes they choose their girlfriend over you (another story for another time).

I was fucked.

Royally fucked.

Gang-bang fucked.

In more ways than one.

I tried my best to keep looking on the bright side and kept telling myself that it would be okay, but that only prolonged the inevitable. I knew what was coming next.

;

It was a mix of everything that sparked off the idea of suicide. I hadn't thought about it in months, and sometimes I completely forgot about it all together but there I was; down in the basement on another dark night, trying to keep my head up high, when all I wanted to do was hang up high.

I didn't have any pills.

Tyler was long gone.

And I had no desire to OD on anything.

I did have a belt, though.

I took my time, making sure that I tied it tight and correctly (the last thing I wanted to do was survive and be brain dead. Yuck!). Even without reading the warnings online, I knew that hanging was a serious gamble, despite being the easiest way to off yourself. If you fucked up before you were dead, then there's a pretty solid chance you'll be eating food through a straw for the rest of your life.

Hence why I took my time.

Once I was sure that I had the noose tight enough and the knot was tied correctly, I started looking around for a place to do it. After some 'research' I learned that there's two types of hanging methods you can use: one with a drop or one without. Obviously, being the lazy prick that I am, I decided to go with the no drop one.

I had one problem, though:

I couldn't find any place to do it in the basement. My bedroom door was made of wood and clearly couldn't support even half of my body weight. There was nothing on the other side of the basement, either.

I remember getting pissed off by this. There I was, trying to commit suicide, and I was unable to. That didn't sit well with me. I didn't give up, though. I kept searching. The closest thing I could get to was the doorknob on my bedroom closet, but it was a big risk since I had no idea how to tie a fucking belt around a doorknob.

But, nevertheless…I gave it a shot.

I tightened the noose, closed part of the belt inside the closet doorway and tested to see if it would fall out or not. It didn't.

Very carefully, I got down on my knees and lifted my head through the opening of the noose until it was just below my chin. My heart was pounding and my face was sweating, but inside I was completely quiet. My mind was coasting and couldn't care less.

I positioned myself.

Took in what was to be my last breath and began to lean forward.

…

I stopped short.

I didn't stop because I had second thoughts or because I wanted to live, I stopped because of mum.

I had put her through so much already, and to force her to make the discovery of me was a really hard thing to just ignore because I knew she would be the one to find my lifeless corpse. The thought brought tears to my eyes almost instantly.

So…instead of going on with it, I took my head out of the noose, pulled the belt out of the doorway, attempted to clear my head and then I went to bed.

Yes, I had chosen not to kill myself that night.

But no, I didn't give up on the idea. In fact, I was more emboldened than ever before. I had done the research, I knew how it was going to go, and I was ready. All I needed to do was find a place to actually do it that wasn't at home.

And it didn't take long at all to find that place.

Back at work, our suite was divided into two separate parts. One part was up on the second floor, and the other was on the first floor. On the first floor, was our own private gym.

The doors to the suite opened at 6:30, but the gym opened at 6:00 and was available for anyone who wanted to use it. The only person that used it that early in the morning was me. Every morning I would be at work right at six and when the badge reader turned green, I would go in and lift a couple weights before I started another wonderfully shitty day.

That was where I decided to do it; in the wee hours of the morning, by myself, with no chance of mum finding my body first (that was some other poor bastards job). When I got the idea, it clicked. But of course, I came up with the idea in the middle of the weekend.

That didn't tamper the mood, though. I overwhelmingly convinced myself that I was going to commit suicide that Monday and nothing could change my mind. I just wanted everything to be over.

Now at this point, you're probably shouting "Stop talking this way, you fucking idiot! Ever heard of permanent solution to temporary problems? Committing suicide is nothing but selfish!"

And you know what I say to that?

FUCK YOU!

Fuck you for thinking that.

Suicide isn't selfish, it's brave.

That's right:

I'll say it again…

SUICIDE IS BRAVE!

And I don't give a shit how offended that makes you because you couldn't be any more wrong.

We don't commit suicide because we're selfish, we do it because we're brave enough to try and stop the pain.

Anyone who says suicide is a cowardly way out is an idiot. There's a big difference between being a coward and being lost. No one knows this better than me because I've been both. Some days I still am.

Now before you slam the book shut, and tell all your friends how much of a horrible human being I am, hear me out.

The physical act of suicide is the dumbest mistake any person can possibly make; that part is undoubtedly true. But the decision to do it is what makes it brave. I say that because some days it's hard to keep your head up; hell some days it's hard just to get up.

Suicide kills you even before you even do anything because the fact that you're even thinking about it is enough to start harming you mentally. Trying to stay positive, putting up a front so no one knows your screaming inside, hoping tomorrow will be better—all this shit takes a lot out of you. It's unimaginable the pain and the mental struggle someone who is thinking about suicide will go through. No one can put that pain into words…not even me.

But the fact that through all of it, all the pain, heartache and let downs, someone can suddenly get to their feet, look themselves in the mirror and decide to say 'no' and fight back is remarkable. You may not agree with the method they choose to fight back with, but you can't deny making a decision like that is far from selfish.

That's why committing suicide is brave. Foolish, but brave.

So before you start judging me, ask yourself if the tables were turned, could you look yourself in the mirror and make that choice? I'm betting you can't.

Hate me all you want, but choosing to fight doesn't make you weak or selfish at all.

That's how I see it now, that's how I saw it years ago.

And that's how I saw it that morning.

;

Like always, the parking lot was empty and so was the building so you can bet your ass as soon as the suit unlocked I was right there to go into the gym. It wasn't a full-blown gym—more like three treadmills and a huge fucking bench press, but still a gym, I guess.

I was laser-focused on just getting it done (probably more than I'd ever been in past suicide attempts). There was a real feel like I was finally going to make it over the hill. Time wasn't on my side though, my co-workers started trickling in at exactly six thirty, I needed to move.

I had been practicing making the noose out of the belt as much as I could so that way as soon as I got in, I could get it done ASAP and I was successful; it must've been up within the first two minutes.

As stupid as it sounds, I was worried it was going to hurt my neck...so I made time to unbutton my black dress up shirt and placed it within the loop (mind over matter, kids).

Then I was set.

Ready to go!

Off to see the wizard.

Everything was in place.

All I needed to do was get on my knees, loop the noose around my neck, do everything in my power not to cry and just lean forward.

Simple as that.

...

I'm sure you're probably waiting for me to say 'I hesitated. I couldn't go through with it because I suddenly saw the good in my life and then realized for the first time in I don't know how long, I didn't wish to be dead.'.

A powerful eye-opening climax that would propel this story to a happy and hopeful conclusion that establishes good times triumph over hard times any day.

That would make a nice conclusion, but nothing like that ever happens in the real world. No dramatic score, no Oscar-winning performance.

This is life.

And life (much like love) is messy.

The truth is I didn't hesitate. I never got a sudden 'life flashing before my eyes' moment. I got to my knees, put my head through the loop, made sure it was tight and then I leaned forward as the brisk morning sunshine shined down on my sweaty face.

The pressure was unimaginable. I felt my face go from pale white to a steaming red in the span of three seconds. Looking back now, I can't remember what I was thinking about in that moment. There's probably a good reason for that and I know I was thinking about something…but I'll be damned if I know.

I could feel my face pulsating in my ears as my vision started to go. From the corner of both eyes, I could see little stars with pure blackness following behind closing in on my pupils. It was actually pretty horrifying if I'm gonna be honest. But that still didn't stop me.

I wasn't going to stop until I was carried out on a fucking stretcher. END OF STORY!

I just did everything I could to resist the overwhelming (and I mean fucking overwhelming) urge to stop and get out while I still could. It might've only taken me about ten to fifteen seconds to pass out from asphyxiation, but they were probably the longest ten to fifteen seconds of my life I shit you not.

I was right there—I could feel it. I had nearly lost all my vision to the stars and blackness and it felt like the vain in my forehead was about to explode. My hands were shaking; my teeth were grinding; saliva was running down my chin (it was quite a sight). If I had to guess, I would say I was at least on the ninth or tenth second.

The moment where everything would stop hurting was right there.

This was it.

I was ready.

No more pain.

No more heartache.

No more anything.

The last thing I remember is my vision going.

;

It was a mix between the morning sunshine and a pulsating headache that brought me out of whatever place I had fallen into. My eyes slowly opened as I adjusted to the sunshine.

I looked around.

Everything had this reddish tint to it.

For a second, I couldn't remember anything. It took me some time before reality sank back in.

I was still in the exercise room.

Still feeling the same.

Still alone.

The sad part is it took me a lot longer than it should've before I realized what the fuck happened (or didn't happen). When I finally lifted myself off my stomach and looked around, I saw for myself.

I shouted.

Screamed.

Then I started weeping.

I had reached a point in my life where no amount of medication, painkillers or illegal drugs would help because there are some things in life that not even medication can help you through.

The worn-out leather belt had split in two, right up the center of my neck, dropping me onto my gut, face down, on the floor, freeing me. Sparing me, in (rather) dramatic fashion.

I was in the exercise room.

Still feeling the same.

Still alone.

Still alive.

I must've laid on that floor for at least an hour, watching the sun come up and watching the sunshine move from my chest to my face. One part of me was furious that I survived yet another attempt while another part felt horrified that I was about a second or two away from actually dying.

I didn't know how to react, or how to feel really.

There was just nothing.

Nothing good.

Nothing bad.

I was split in two.

Much like the belt resting at my feet.

12/31/2014

Another year gone.

Definetly some highs and definetly some lows. Not sure how I'll feel when I think about 2014 in the future. Not the best year, but not the worst year. So many people are gone though.

Normally don't get deep into new year resolutions but Im hoping for a miracle next year. It would be nice if something actually worked out without having to jump threw hoops to get there. Guess you could call that my new years resolution.

And finding someone would be a nice change to. It gets boring going to bed by yourself everynight. I'm going to really try this year so maybe something along the way can meet me in the middle.

Might be to much to ask for but time will tell I guess.

Until next time

;

There are moments in life that come up unexpectedly that end up shaping you for a very long ass time; maybe for the rest of your life.

For some people it's abuse.

Others addiction.

The fucking list is a mile long.

For me, it wasn't the abuse from my father or my struggles with drug addiction.

For me it was suicide.

I had taken my life for granted for so long, I forgot what it was like to live. Now I'll be the first to admit, I would love to sit here and tell you that the nearly successful suicide attempt changed my life and I saw life in a whole new light and suddenly for the first time in I don't know how long, I realized I didn't wish to be dead...but I can't.

But that's not as depressing as it seems.

Yes, I still wished life was over.

Yes, I was still depressed to the point of no return.

Yes, I basically lost all hope.

But that moment in the gym was the last time I ever attempted suicide.

Maybe it triggered something, maybe it didn't, but whatever the case may be, looking at it now, I think it's fair to say that was one of those moments that came up unexpectedly that ended up shaping me for a very long time; maybe for the rest of my life.

;

The weeks that followed were nothing short of fucking miserable. My tolerance level was nonexistent and my sleeping habits were in a league of their own (to put it lightly).

I would go a solid three or four days without any type of real sleep and then finally on the fifth day I would sleep like a rock. My dreams, though, were always fucked up nightmares. What made sense in another realm ended up being nothing more than broken pieces of frames that had no relevance. It reminded me of my more glory days abusing narcotics.

In those few wonderful weeks, while I tried fighting every urge in me to do something stupid, I learned a few things that ended up being rather valuable pieces of info even to this very day.

First: addiction is lifelong.

You can go days, weeks, months, years, decades without so much as thinking about relapsing, but when the shit hits the fan (and it always does soon or later, just give it time) it's very tempting to do a complete 180 in a split second. And anyone who thinks differently has clearly not fully recovered from addiction. What takes years to build up can be destroyed in seconds.

Second: Problems are still there even when you're not.

That one might be a little confusing so I'll rephrase that: just because I would get drunk or do oxy or decide I wanted to become an amputee doesn't change the fact that I'm gay. Or the fact that I was in love with someone who I knew I'd never be with. Eventually, at some point, the buzz wears off and the drugs get flushed out of your system and the problems/ issues are still there greeting you with a great big smile.

We're all different and we all go through some pretty slimy shit, but trying to medicate it away doesn't work. I know, I was disappointed too. Maybe that'll help you, maybe it won't, but at least you've been warned, if nothing else.

And finally (finally!) the last thing: don't lie to yourself.

Basic.

Simple.

But the most important thing of the three.

I'll be the first to agree with you that bullshitting yourself is tempting and why shouldn't it be? You have all these problems and feelings in life and you need a way to escape them, right?

WRONG!

We don't become something ugly because we need a way to escape things, we become ugly because we've already faced them and don't like the end result. That's just a fact.

Listen, if you want to lie to everyone else, do what you have to do; some fucker like me isn't going to stop you or change your mind, but don't lie to yourself. Sooner or later you'll start believing them and that just adds another layer of shit to the pile you already have to deal with.

Take my word for it.

;

Back then, that "experience" in the gym was nothing more than another failed attempt to do something so simple (another notch in the belt). I was disappointed, yet again, because for some unknown reason, every time I pulled the trigger nothing would happen. Who would've thought killing yourself would be such a hard thing to do?

It's fucking depressing to admit, but I think I was so disappointed in myself that I never tried another attempt after that, because I didn't want to let myself down again (no pun intended).

I just decided to keep going.

Day by day.

Little by little.

Hoping that at some point I could get back to where I was…or close to it.

There were a bunch of times around this point where I gave serious thought to coughing up and telling mum what was going on. I came close to it, too. But the fear of that good old padded room on Shutter Island left that idea untouched. That also got me thinking about what would happen if I coughed up to Ledner.

Basically, to put it simply: I was stuck.

Stuck in a fucking rut.

It was not fun at all, but toward the end of the first week and as my appointment with Ledner drew closer, another drug overdose caught my attention and shifted the ground beneath me.

Only this time, it wasn't one I was a part of.

;

As mentioned before, when I started doing an obscene amount of illegal drugs (with a touch of alcohol mixed in on occasion), I dug a hole and buried in deep, isolating myself. Drug addiction is a lonely business. But as it turned out, I wasn't the only one who decided to hunker down, many followed suit.

The first 'down to earth' moment for me happened when I was at the store one day after work. I looked and felt like one of the zombies from the walking dead so I didn't think much of it, but while in line, a familiar voice rang in my ears.

"Hey, Matt."

It took a second for me to pull my head out of my ass, but when I did I saw it was Mike; an old classmate that I hadn't seen since graduation way the fuck back in 2010.

"How are ya?"

I forced out a smile. "I'm fine, how're you?"

To be honest I tuned him out pretty much after that. He went on and on, bragging about how he landed some job working for a lawyer and was getting ready to make bank as soon as he got out of school. It got annoying fast, in all honesty.

At that point in my life, I had somehow managed to cobble up some cash and self-publish my first book a few months' back, so as he kept going on and on about how excited he was with life, I gave serious thought about doing the same to him…but I didn't.

I let him have the moment.

It was painfully obvious that he wanted to use up some bragging rights he figured he had. I wasn't in the mood to listen to him, let alone talk about what it's like being a 'published author'.

Back in high school, he was one of only a handful of openly gay guys at our school. For a brief (and I mean brief) moment, we were talking to each other, but it amounted to nothing. Probably my fault, but there was no chemistry let alone attraction, so I just stopped talking to him altogether. I assume that had a little to do with his whole braggadocios attitude, so I figured I probably deserved it anyway.

We talked (well he talked) up until he paid for his shit and then left. The last thing I said to him was "I'm glad things are going good for you. I'm happy for you."

"Thanks, have a good one."

That was it.

Thought nothing else of it.

Paid for my shit and went back to my hiding spot, deep in the basement of my house.

I didn't think much about it after really. I mean I was happy that he was getting someplace good in life, but outside of a couple laughs and jokes I told him, we hardly knew each other from a hole in the wall.

But I was more than surprised when I learned he died not even three months after.

I was in my basement going through my news feed when I found out. We weren't friends on Facebook, but I was mutual friends with many of his and everything they said all pointed to suicide.

That was a tough visual, not to mention it didn't make much sense since he seemed to have his life somewhat intact. Course that doesn't mean shit now does it? I think I proved that a couple dozen pages back.

Again, we were far from close, but his death bothered me.

Really bothered me.

More than it should've, I guess.

It would be another couple of weeks before I found out how he really died.

It wasn't a suicide. Well, not intentionally I don't think.

It was a drug overdose.

Didn't see that one coming.

At all.

I never heard it directly from his family but from the sounds of one of his very close friends, he had a problem for a very long time. I guess since just after high school. The story is, he was having issues with his boyfriend and needed a break from reality.

He was found in a hotel bathroom.

Pronounced dead at the scene.

Again, a tough visual to think about.

It was right around the time of Mike's death when I finally started to see how shut off I'd become from the world. It was pretty eye-opening, actually. I had become so focused on trying to stay clean, plus juggling a secret relationship I wasn't supposed to be in, that I allowed the rest of the world to pass by like a bad dream. It was a wakeup call.

That was when I decided I would come out of my dark basement and reestablish contact with many of the people I'd left behind years ago.

I had no idea the shit I was about to find out.

;

Dead.

Many—if not most of them were dead.

One of them: crashed into a tree

Another: hit by a drunk driver

Another: murdered

Two more: suicide

Another: heart attack

Another: hit and run

And finally five of them: drug overdoses

In between graduation and the end of 2014-early 2015, I had lost a dozen plus friends and acquaintances, all of them under the age of 25. All under my nose, right before my eyes, but paid no attention to it. It was nothing short of gut-wrenching.

Some I had known from banging into them in halls, others I'd known from being in the same classes and a few of them I truly called friends.

All of them: gone.

Some for a while, too.

It was devastating.

I hadn't cried since my last suicide attempt, but that changed when I saw so many people had moved on. It's hard saying goodbye to one person you know. It's impossible to say goodbye to nearly a dozen you know. And all at the same time.

Child abuse changed me.

Falling in love with a straight guy changed me.

Drug abuse changed me.

Bipolar changed me.

And that night changed me.

Because I learned on that very long night: time flies when you take your eyes off the clock.

Many of my friends learned that the hard way.

And so did I.

The only difference was I was still alive.

11/6/2015

Wow! Does the fucking time fly! So much has happened since Dec 2014!

Still on meds and still see Ledner but everything is stable as of today. Been feeling really good,

Got two books published with a third on the way! Thank god they arent kids. Its funny looking back because I remember where I was when I wrote a few of these but not others. This past summer May-August 2015 was one of the best summers because I might've found somebody. Not sure what I enjoyed most about this past summer: meeting someone knew or getting hope for something I had. Course now its basically over but wheather good times or bad times lie a head, all I can say is I loved this past summer and I hope I get more of them. Until next time⋯

;

Couldn't help but laugh reading this.

I actually remember writing this one.

I was in a good place. The love life, if you can call it a love life, was going good. Even saw hope in the distance that maybe shit was going to turn out alright between the two of us…but that's a story for another time (maybe).

The big deal here was that I remember feeling stable when I wrote this. Life wasn't in chaos, I wasn't depressed and I wasn't thinking about any form of relapse. I had moved on, well as much as an addict can move on to be fair.

But like the other times, it was a fucking miserable, goddamn, mother fucking, climb to get there!

;

Jumping back to the early days of 2015 (time travel!), I was still pretty much a fucking basket case. That span between me being out of pills and seeing Ledner again was the worst, but slowly the days added up and finally it was time for me to go see the little weirdo and ask for more refills so I could get back on track.

I didn't tell mum about my 'cold turkey' gig with my meds and in the end, I didn't tell Ledner, either. If he would've asked then maybe I would've said something, but all he did was give me a few pages of refills and that was it. Our session couldn't have been more than a half-hour, at best.

The first thing I needed to do was build the lithium back up in my system, because that was the wonder drug that kept me sane. But overdosing on prescription pills wasn't exactly the best way to make sure I had it in my system, so I improvised.

Yes, you're about to get mad at me again.

…

…

Sorry.

But if you're not used to that by now, then I may not be the only one that has problems here.

Anyway, I did some research online and finally was able to find this website that detailed every medication you couldn't take with lithium and how each would interact if you did.

There are 1,166 different medications that interact with lithium.

Yes, one thousand one hundred and sixty-six.

Now, to be fair, only 266 of them have severe interactions. If you want to consider that as a silver lining, feel free to do so. I did.

Those 266 interactions are what I focused on first. Some of the interactions were pretty obvious: lithium and Percocet or lithium and valium don't mix well. Any idiot could probably figure that out on their own, but some of the others were as obvious.

Probably the biggest shocker of them all was ibuprofen. Not only did it interact, it was a DANGEROUS interaction. Reading deeper into it, apparently, ibuprofen can spike up the lithium dose in the body to dangerous levels if enough is taken.

Didn't see that one coming, but didn't overlook it, either. In fact, I used that information to my advantage (told you that you were probably gonna be mad at me again).

Because it had been so long since I had taken any medication, I knew I needed to do something to jump start it in my system and since doubling up on pills didn't seem like a smart approach given my 'past behavior', I did decide to take another risk and ended up mixing lithium and ibuprofen.

Yes, I was aware that is was risky.

Yes, I was aware that it could lead to that all too familiar rabbit hole.

But I convinced myself that it was for the greater good and in a skewed sense, it was. I knew they needed to be at 'therapeutic levels', so I was just trying to give them a little boost.

I was cautious and made sure I kept it very limited, but I believed and felt confident that I was doing the right thing.

I didn't tell anyone, actually never have until now about that.

But it did work.

It wasn't a two-week gap like every other time. It was close to it, but a day or two less, is still a day or two less.

And this time I stayed on them. I disciplined myself in a way that I'd never done so before because I told myself I never wanted to go back to that dark place I was at again.

I wanted to try to feel normal.

I wanted that level feeling that I had at one point and I was hell-bent to get it and keep it.

I may have done it in a fucked up way, but finally, I got there and that would set up a solid foundation for 2015, which was easily one of my more better years in life even if it didn't last all year.

;

"Why me?" I asked Ledner during one of our only handful of sessions in 2015. "Why am I still here and so many others aren't?"

"Not sure I know the answer to that," Ledner said bluntly. "Maybe you're here for a reason or maybe you just have good luck and they didn't."

"Wow, you probably don't have many friends do you?"

"Nope, I do my job and go home."

Another failed attempt at trying to prove Ledner was human, but that question was on my mind a lot. Of course Ledner really wasn't the person to get all philosophical with. If it wasn't done by the book, he wanted no part of it. He was honest, though. I've got to give him that.

"So I'm going to extend our session out pretty long. You seem to be doing really well, surprisingly. Your labs are good, you clearly aren't doing any illegal drugs and you actually seem to be pretty happy."

"Wish I could say the same to you."

"I'm going to put our next meeting out until next year. Obviously, if you have any problems, contact me and you can come in sooner, but other than that, I think you're doing well."

Despite still not showing any signs of life, Ledner's words were very encouraging. If I remember correctly, I think I even shook his hand when I left his creepy ass office (yes, his planets were still dead).

"See you next year."

And just like that, Ledner was gone for the foreseeable future. I knew I was going to miss him like a decaying tooth and I'm sure the feeling was probably mutual. There's no denying I owed him big for pushing me in the right direction, but aside from that, there was nothing else. It's not like we were heading toward a Good Will Hunting bond where we hated each other at first and then become best friends forever.

We just never had that.

Not a bad thing, I guess.

;

Not having to worry about seeing Ledner was a big monkey off my back, because that meant I didn't need to worry as much about my meds. If I just stayed on track, I would be fine. He told me that dozens of times and this time I was really going to try it.

But having all this free time and lack of monkeys allowed my mind to clear up and start asking one very simple question over and over:

WHY THE FUCK WAS I STILL ALIVE?

WHY?

WHY?

WHY?

Why did I live and so many others didn't?

So many of them had such a bright future.

And all of them were much better people than me. I'm rude, selfish and demanding. All of them were kind, caring and selfless.

It made no sense why they were all gone and I, somehow, was still roaming the Earth like a fucking cockroach that was too stubborn to die.

It was hard to think about them in the past tense. It was even harder to try and convince myself that they were now in a place that many say exists high up in the sky somewhere.

Call me a non-believer, but I'm not a religious person. I don't believe in God, or some type of afterlife. I wish I did, because somedays it probably would help ease some of the tension that builds up in life, but I just don't. I do believe in UFOs though, if that counts for anything.

But wherever they are, I hope they're at peace. They all deserve it. Their families do, too. So maybe that can be considered as believing in something, I'll let you make that call.

Now, one would assume that this is the part where I suddenly find the reason why the universe took so many great people but left me alive. That I found my moral calling, where I take everything I learned during my journey of self-destruction and find some way to use it for the greater good.

Come full circle, learn the error of my ways and try to be an inspiration for all who are willing to listen?

That would be awesome, right?

THAT'S RIGHT!

That's exactly what this is all about.

To prove I've grown as a person and that I'm no longer this evil little man who died inside years ago!

I'm a new man!

. . .

. . .

Gotcha!

You didn't think the story was heading towards that kind of ending, did you?

The type of ending where the sun shines bright and the stars all aligned? Come on! You know better than that by now! Or at least you should.

Besides we're not at the ending yet (getting close, however).

No, this is not the part where I transform from some half past dead former drug user/ bipolar sufferer/ fag to this bright city on a hill that everyone can point to and say 'he made it'. Sorry to disappoint if that's what you were rooting for.

This is the point, however where I finally decided to come out of my shell and rejoin the world and reach out; specifically to the people I left behind all those years ago.

I knew it was going to be hard because I wasn't the same person I was and so much had changed, but I felt almost obligated to somehow try and reemerge back into society and eventually try to fix some of the wrongs I'd done.

It was easier said than done, though.

Yes, at this point I knew I had learned from everything I'd gone through, but just because you get through something, doesn't mean you're completely over it.

Now, I might've lost a handful of you so I'll explain:

Surviving suicide, is a big deal.

Surviving drug abuse, is a big deal.

Struggling with mental illness, is a big deal.

Finding a way to hold onto hope about a relationship that deep down you know could fail at any second, is a big deal.

But living with that shit; more importantly, talking about that shit, is not as easy as just licking your wounds and calling it a day. Admitting what you are and what you've done are two entirely separate things.

Why?

Because people suck ass!

Most importantly: people judge.

And not one of us can call it out and say that it's wrong because we've all done it at some point. I'll proudly be the first to admit it.

Now, I think we'd all like to try to find the positive side of everything and times are changing where people are SLOWLY starting to realize drug abuse is more of an illness than a crime...but we're still not there.

Not yet, anyway.

Some of you may not believe that.

Some you of might think that we have reached the point where we can pat each other on the back instead of slap on handcuffs. And if you are one of those people, good for you. I won't even make fun of you because the world could actually use a couple million more of you.

But experience triumphs over hope every time and I have experience, so don't get mad when I say, as a country, we are not there yet.

To be honest, I don't think I'm there yet, either.

I don't consider myself a criminal who deserves to be in jail, but there are those days that pop up where I feel weak because I've spent so much time and energy trying to resist those tiny little pills while, the rest of the world carried on. That's where my head is now and that's where it was back then when I decided I would start to make contact again.

It was time to face reality, and see what else was waiting on the other side.

9/13/2016

Back again.

Like I said before, it doesn't feel like so much time has past since the last time I was here. Its still scary to think about but I guess when you think about it all of us are born to die.

The year has been a little challenging, but nothing I haven't felt with before.

Relationship life is still out of whack and some days, many days have been pretty lonely, but that all changed today so maybe 2016 can end on a high note. We'll see what happens.

Lost a few more people this year. Starting to think that's going to get common as I get deeper in life. Also scary to think about when you take the time to do so. Maybe 2017 will be different.

I'm not sure if I'll get back to this before the end of the year or at all actually. Lifes been moving pretty quick, but if I don't I want to say that aside from the love life, things feel okay.

It been a long road, but its nice to know that I'm not alone in the end and haven't been. Been thinking about possibly trying to write about all the shit I gone threw in all these years again but not sure where or how to start. Last time didn't work out like I was hoping so we'll see what happens.

Maybe.

Until next time.

;

The final entry.

The final entry on a long 'journey'.

For those of you who have somehow stayed on this far, maybe you'll be able to stay with me a little longer. I'll keep it brief for those with a short attention span, like myself.

;

You know how you get that feeling, when you remember something you said or did and when you realize how long ago it actually was, you're really surprised because it doesn't feel like it's been that long?

That's what this last entry feels like.

I know it's not 4-5 years ago but still just far enough along where I looked at it and said 'damn'.

Anyway, remember way the hell back in the beginning of all this I said something along the lines of 'drug abuse is like war, because it changes you' (it was worded differently, but I'm too lazy to go back and look for the exact quote, but you get the gist)?

Well, keep that in mind as you read the rest of this.

;

Despite wanting to reach out, I didn't rush into it. I gave the idea time to nest and made sure I was confident that it was something I really wanted to do. If there was one thing I learned on this journey of self-inflicting wounds, it was that sometimes the past is better left behind. That alone was enough to halt me in my tracks and seriously question what was going to happen next.

I thought about it for months and yet I was still torn about what the hell to do. There was no doubt that I wanted closure on many things I started and never finished, but many times the closure you want isn't the closure you end up getting. It was hard to get over that.

It got to the point where I was completely stuck and I had no fucking idea what I wanted to, or even should do. I was hesitant to ask for advice because I knew what many people's answers would end up being, but it ate away at me so much, that in the end, I did crack.

I ended up asking for advice from someone I never thought I would.

;

"And what made you decide you want to reach out?" Ledner asked me in what will be his final appearance in this story.

Despite the usual flatness in his voice, I actually really thought about what the answer was. In a way, I had an answer, but to find the right words to explain it was fucking difficult for some reason. I resorted to my normal "I don't know."

"Uh huh...and what do you expect to get out of reaching out?"

"Peace, maybe?" I suggested with sarcasm.

He kept writing everything down. "You normally don't find much peace when you interact with people you've hurt, but I won't mention that."

"Well, it's better than doing nothing."

"There's several theories to that, but you still haven't answered my question: what do you expect to get out of this?"

"I don't know. Why is everything with you so goddamn micromanaged?" I nearly yelled, fully embracing the fact that I wanted Ledner to know he was pissing me off, fast.

"Again, you still haven't given me an answer."

"What the fuck do you want me to say? Is there some special answer I'm supposed to give you to prove that I'm a better person now than I was when I first walked into this shitty office? Well, I'm sorry, but I don't know what that answer is. This is something I feel like I should do. Yes, I know it's risky because of everything, but there's things I need to fix before I can move on. And I'm sorry if you're so out of touch with reality that you don't understand that...and get rid of these goddamn plants! They're fucking depressing to look at!"

For once, Ledner actually looked up at me. Just like the last time I yelled at him and called him a fucking idiot, I could feel my face turning bright red and start pulsating. I went back to looking at the clock across the room, watching the seconds tick away, wishing I was somewhere else.

Ledner went back to writing and I went back to rolling my eyes. As usual, it was hard to figure out what Ledner was thinking. His face was flat and he remained calm (just like last time).

A solid five minutes must've gone by without either of us saying a fucking word to each other. The sound of his pencil moving across the paper was worse than fucking nails on a chalkboard. I gave serious thought to throwing one of his dead plants at him.

"I think you should do it," he suddenly said.

I was confused. "What?"

"I think you should go and reach out."

I was still confused. "Two seconds ago, you were saying I shouldn't."

"Actually I never said that. I was going to say it before, but you were busy talking about my quote un-quote fucking depressing plants."

I didn't say shit to him at first because after thinking about it, he was right. He never did say that; I just assumed he would think it was a bad idea, given he's never acted human in all the years I saw him.

"Oh, why do you think I should?"

Again, while he kept on writing, he answered. "Because you are a different person than you were when you first started coming here. I'm still not changing my conclusion that you have a short fuse, don't think when you say things and overact like a child, but you have changed. A few years ago, I would've disapproved of your reaching out theory, but given where you are now, I think it's appropriate to do so."

"Really?" I said shell-shocked.

Still trying to process the almost kind words he said, I watched Ledner open up the yellow file he had on the top of his desk, pulled out a completely filled page from the back and handed it to me.

Both sides of the page were written on, it looked like a fucking essay some poor bastard in college was stuck writing, but the nearly perfect handwriting was easy to read.

Right on the top of the page was: 'Subject brought in after second suicide attempt. Possible signs of mental illness up to but not limited to Bipolar I, II or rapid cycle.'

The page was dated over four years back.

Now there was so much shit written on it that I only had time to glance through it, but as I sped through it, it was almost as if I was reading about someone who was nothing but a stranger, nothing but a 'subject' I'd never met. It took a moment for me to remember I was reading about myself.

"Holy shit," I muttered just loud enough for Ledner to hear I guess.

"Still think you're the same person?"

For the first time in a long time, I was at a loss for words. I couldn't even force anything out even if I wanted to. Looking back I wish I did say something, but I stayed silent and listened to Ledner talk a bit about my meds and push out our next meeting to over a year.

I agreed and left.

At this point, some of you people (still reading this long and uneventful story) might be saddened that Ledner and I would never end up having the 'connection' you hear about when a psychiatrist has a difficult patient they're forced to deal with, but like I said dozens of times, life isn't always perfect.

But after that session, I remember thinking for a second maybe somewhere deep down, past all the awkwardness, maybe Ledner had a little touch of humanity in him after all.

Maybe.

;

After getting Ledner's 'approval' about my idea, I did finally rejoin society as a clean (ish) addict. The past was still clinging to me like a fresh corpse, but for the most part, I was able to ignore it enough where I could try and move on.

I started reaching out.

But it couldn't be just anyone.

The first person I needed to reach out to was someone I knew would be honest and get straight to the point.

Someone who had a right to be angry with me.

Someone that had something that I never finished.

And that person was a friend of mine named Nick.

Nick and I had met my senior year of high school. At first, he hated me because I always harassed his girlfriend Beth, but over time I wore him down and we ended up being good friends, for a while.

Nick was one of only a handful of people I stayed in contact with when I first started abusing drugs, but over time, just like everyone else, I pulled away and stopped hanging out with him and his girl.

It had been close to five years since he and I last spoke to each other. It had been ever longer since the last time we had a face to face, so if anyone would give me a sense of what reaching out was going to be like, it was going to be him.

So I did.

I reached out.

...

And so did he.

I'd be lying if I said I wasn't shitting my pants when he responded. You could say that the last time we saw each other, it didn't end very well (that's all you need to know and all you're going to get).

Like I said many times throughout this fucking book, time takes away everything and my hope was that for once, it would take away something negative. Of course I wasn't holding my breath.

But as it turned out, time actually did me a favor. It did end up taking something away that I wanted and needed it to. Time is a fucking asshole, but sometimes it actually helps. Sometimes.

We must've talked for hours before and after we met up to grab something to eat. Aside from being a little older, wiser and hotter, something was different about him. I couldn't place what the fuck it was, but I knew there was something. I could see it in his eyes (not trying to sound dramatic, but it was true).

His eyes looked 'healthy' like they were full of life in a way that I'd never seen them. And as it so happens, I learned I wasn't the only one on a journey of self-destruction.

It's not my story to tell, but let's say him and I could relate to a lot of things. My jaw dropped lower and lower with every word he said.

It was absolutely devastating to hear. I always told him he was going to be someone and to hear how far he veered off the track, brought a tear to my eye. I couldn't believe it. When I got home after hanging out, I cried because the things he told me were so horrifying.

But despite everything he went through, he cleaned himself up, straightened out his life and got back on that path to being someone. I never have and never will forget that night because it was that night when I learned its okay to be flawed. He taught me that and it stuck with me. It still does. In this story, Nick is that person you can point to and say 'he did it' because he really did and it was awesome to see.

Not every experience was like that, though.

There were some who could never forgive me for what I said and did to them back in the day. I can't say I blame them, either. I was a fucking asshole back before I was diagnosed with Bipolar. The crude and disgusting things I did and said hurt people, pissed off many and broke up a lot of relationships.

There were some who never responded, but it made me feel better knowing I did my part, not sure what else to say about that. I like to think they at least read what I had to say, if nothing else.

There were others who didn't respond because they were gone. Several of them had also passed way too soon; some of them very dramatically. Nick was able to relate to that, too.

And then there were some who not only ended up responding, but also started getting back in touch with me. It seemed like, out of the blue, one by one we began coming out of the rabbit hole we all fell into and rejoined reality. It was almost surreal because of how organic it was.

;

Something started happening the more I reached out. I didn't pick up on it or even notice it right away, to be honest. It was so in synch that I couldn't even see what was building up right in front of me; what was forming right in front of me. But over time it kept building up to the point where it ended up hitting me like a bullet at point-blank range.

We all came from different backgrounds.

Some of us were guys.

Some of us were girls.

Some white, some black.

Some in college, some still living at home.

But despite the diversity of us all, we had two things in common:

We were all around the same age.

And we all were recovering from drug addiction.

I was speechless.

For years, I had always thought I fell into the rabbit hole by myself and during the time I was down there, everyone else kept living life and moved on from who we were back in high school. In all that time, I never thought for a second that anyone else had fallen into the rabbit hole.

But I was wrong.

Very wrong.

I wasn't the only one.

There were MANY of us.

It was surreal.

Even now it's hard to put into words what exactly it felt like, but I guess the best analogy would be this:

My grandfather served in Vietnam in 1969. As a Sergeant in the 101st Airborne, it was his job to lead his men into battle.

One of those battles was 'Hamburger Hill'.

Some find the name of the hill humorous, but it actually got its name because so many American soldiers were slaughtered. Their bodies were so chewed up, they looked like chopped meat mixed in the mud. It was one of the bloodiest battles in Vietnam.

600 men went up.

Less than one third came down.

My grandpa was part of that one third. He made it to the top. And when I heard all the stories about what he went through, I imagined him standing at the top of the hill late at night, surrounded by smoke and looking down at the stragglers emerging through it, trying to figure out who was going home and who wasn't.

Me reaching out and finding out about so many of us one by one was my Hamburger Hill moment. I made it to the top and now came the part where I had to look back down and see who was behind me and who was lost in the smoke.

My grandpa lost friends, I lost friends.

My grandpa nearly died, I nearly died.

My grandfather was never the same when he came home, I was never the same when I came home. That vision has stayed with me over the years and even now I think about it. Every time I hear about someone who died of an OD, I get sad because I know that means another one isn't going to emerge from the smoke.

I may never know exactly what my grandfather went through back in Vietnam, all those years ago, but I have an idea. I really do.

1/5/2018

2:17

It always seems like I get back here at the beginning of the year with every intention to write in here more and somehow I never seem to have the time to do it. Hell, I didn't even write in this last year! I'd say I'm going to really (really) try to write in here more, but there's a pretty solid chance this will be the first and only entry for 2018.

Like always: a lot has happened since last time.

Yes, I'm still confused about the whole 'relationship' thing.

Yes, I'm still taking ten thousand different types of medication.

Yes, I still see Ledner

Yes, to a lot of things; nearly all of them are good.

But there is one 'No'. And it's not a 'no' I think many might think it would be. Or one that anybody is going to like.

I'd love to write in here that its been so and so many years that I've been this or so and so many years since that and everything bad has been left behind. But it hasn't. Truth is I haven't been clean for years or even a year or even half a year.

Or even a month.

Or even a week.

The truth is some of that shit I talked about before came back up in life that I wasn't prepared for. I let my guard down and I was weak and I relapsed.

It hasn't been easy. It never is, but I'm not as far in the rabbit hole as I once was. I know where I am and I know what I have to do to get back on track.

With the exception of the last three months, 2017 was by far one of the best years of my life. It ended shitty without question, but I have hopes for 2018 and I think I'm gonna be okay. That's not me trying to blow smoke up your ass, either.

I've gotten to my feet once before and I know I'll get there again. It's not a question of how, just a question of when. Like I've always said: I don't believe in happily ever after's, but I do believe in hope.

;

...

...

...

Well, not the storybook ending, huh? At least not yet, anyway.

I know some of you might be surprised and even a little upset by how this is shaping up to end. Believe me, no one is more surprised by it than me. But maybe that's not hard to believe given my past experiences or entries).

I actually have tears in my eyes writing this because of how I'm going to have to end this. Normally this would be the part in the movie or TV show (or a typical book for that matter) where things settle down, everything works out and the protagonist gets ready to head off into the sunset.

But like I said many times before: I'm not a hero in this story.

...

...

I really do wish I could've been the guy some of you thought I might've or should've ended up being in these last couple pages. I'm sorry I can't sit here and tell you that I am, but as I said in the beginning: life can be messy. Life IS messy.

I failed, and I failed myself. That's something I have to live with for a very long time. Reading this, you may be feeling sad or even sympathy, but don't. It's a waste of my time and yours.

Truth is this isn't as sad as some might think.

I know I fucked up, but I'm still here and I'm still chugging along with no intention of stopping anytime soon.

Some of you might also be thinking that you're doomed to repeat yourself like I did.

But my story isn't your story. If there's one thing I learned from all this, it's that I'm not alone. We're not alone.

There are millions of us out there.

We each have our own story.

And we each get to choose what happens in the story.

And we all get to choose what happens NEXT in the story.

I was kind of hoping not to end this in some boring motivational speech where I tell all of you (who can relate to even a fraction of the shit I mentioned), that it gets better because of how corny and overused that type of ending is.

But I guess it's a better ending than saying 'thank you for listening! Now fuck off and go back to your own life.'

...

I guess.

;

JUST KIDDING!!!

That's exactly how I'm going to end this, because that's exactly what you should be doing! Life's too short to sit back and let it pass by for Christ sakes (you have more problems than I do if you haven't figured that out yet)!

Yes, addiction is hard.

Yes, being gay is hard.

Yes, dealing with mental illness is hard.

But just because it's hard, doesn't mean it's impossible. If you take away any advice from this shitty-ass story, I want it to be this:

1: Put this goddamn book down

2: Walk over to the closest mirror

3: (Before it breaks) Look yourself in the eyes

4: Figure out who's looking at you

5: Figure out who you want looking at you

6: Realize; despite all the flaws, that you can be that person

7: Go outside

8: Be that person.

Period.

The only light at the end of the tunnel is the one we create for ourselves.

And with that, this is where I'm going to leave you. From the bottom of my little black heart, I want you to know how honored I am that you've allowed me to take you on this journey. I hope it's given you something to think about, if nothing else.

So…with that said:

Thank you for listening! Now fuck off and get back to your own life!

☺

-Matt

.

Made in the USA
Las Vegas, NV
28 December 2023

83662232R00069